For Ever and Ever

Book Three
of the Enduring Faith Series

SUSAN C. FELDHAKE

ZondervanPublishingHouse
Grand Rapids, Michigan

A Division of HarperCollinsPublishers

For Ever and Ever
Copyright © 1993 by Susan C. Feldhake

Requests for information should be addressed to:
Zondervan Publishing House
Grand Rapids, Michigan 49530

Library of Congress Cataloging in Publication Data

Feldhake, Susan C.
   For Ever and Ever / Susan C. Feldhake
     p.   cm. – (Enduring faith series : bk. 3)
   ISBN 0-310-48131-7 (pbk.)
  I. Title. II. Series: Feldhake, Susan C. Enduring faith series : bk. 3.
PS3556.E4575F58   1993
813'.54—dc20   92-36299
                                                CIP

Edited by Anne Severance
Cover design by Jody Langley
Illustrations by Bob Sabin

Printed in the United States of America

94 95 96 97 98 99 00 01 02 / DH / 12 11 10 9 8 7 6 5 4 3 2

For my dear parents,
Arvid and Millie Christiansen,
of Williams, Minnesota,
who celebrated their 50th wedding anniversary
on June 12, 1991,
and serve as a shining example of
"for ever and ever" . . .

chapter
1

"I NOW PRONOUNCE you man and wife," said the beaming parson.

"Hallelujah!" cried a jubilant Lizzie. Grabbing her new husband, she gave him an enthusiastic buss full on the lips before turning a radiant face on the cluster of family and friends gathered to witness their vows in the parlor of her Salt Creek cabin. "I purely thought this day would never come!"

Her passionate outburst brought a ripple of laughter from the amused onlookers who moved forward to kiss the bride and pump the groom's hand.

"My, but you're purty as a picture today, Miss Lizzie," said old Mr. Gartner, who owned the neighboring farm down the road a piece. "If you wasn't already spoke for, I'd be tempted to ask you myself!"

"Why, you look more like a schoolgirl than the mother of three strappin' sons!" came a complaint from a plump matron.

Hearing the reluctant compliment, Lizzie smiled. She knew she looked her best today, or at least as well as an old woman of twenty-three could look! She'd washed and ironed her best dress—a flower-sprigged dimity that Jem especially liked—and she'd done up her long hair in a loose knot at the nape of her neck. Not that it would stay up for long. Already a few wild tendrils had sprung from the confining pins and tumbled to her shoulders. Even so, she'd seen the loving approval in Jeremiah's eyes when he'd first seen her, and if Jem was happy—she was happy!

Moving outside, Fanchon Preston supervised the spreading of her daughter's wedding feast on makeshift plank tables set up beneath the maple trees in the side yard.

"'Tis a fine day for a weddin'!" called her husband, Will, whose old bones were aching and prevented his doing much more on this busy day than tending their infant granddaughter, Harmony.

Fanny looked about in relief. Thank goodness, it wasn't raining. Only last week, it had poured cats and dogs. That and the unseasonably warm spell that followed had brought out the wildflowers now perfuming the air. Pert dandelions, snugged low to the ground, lifted their yellow faces to duplicate the blazing sun overhead. And in the distance, the rugged hillsides of this central Illinois region were resplendent with towering hardwood trees just beginning to unfurl their tightly clenched leaves, preparing to shade the good earth from summer's fierce heat.

Soon other neighbors from the close-knit Salt Creek community arrived in their Sunday best, the women filing by to offer the finest wares from their kitchens to contribute to the meal. Clinging to their mamas' skirts were the youngest children, spit-and-polished, while the older ones lit out for the nearest climbing tree or played tag in the newly lush grasses of the nearby meadow. Trailing in their wake came the menfolk, hailing each other and pausing in congenial groups to chat about crops and weather as well as the joyous event that had given them a rare holiday from their labors.

With all their friends looking on, Jeremiah and Lizzie cut the cake that was Fanny's work of art, fed each other bites of the succulent treat, then retired to an area reserved for them. As if on cue, the guests passed through the serving line and seated themselves on blankets or on the flatbeds of wagons.

The afternoon passed quickly and enjoyably until dusk began to drape the landscape in violet shadows. Those families with young children or livestock to feed prepared to leave for home early.

Patiently Alton stood in line holding the twins, Molly and Marissa, one in each arm, while a tired and cranky Katie clung to his leg.

"Pa Wheeler!" Lizzie cried, hoisting herself onto her tiptoes to plant a kiss on his bearded cheek. "I'm right proud to be a part of your fam'ly, I am! And I hope to be a daughter you can delight in."

"Remember, you're not losin' your boy, Alton, but gainin' a daughter," Fanny chimed in, giving his arm a comforting pat. "Can't help thinkin' Sue Ellen would be mightily pleased with this pairin', too. She was always as partial to our Lizzie as we've been fond of Jem."

Lizzie noticed the mingling of pain and pleasure on her new pa-in-law's face at the mention of his beloved late wife and hurried to bridge the awkward moment.

"Just because Jem 'n' I are married now doesn't mean you'll be seein' less of him, Pa Wheeler. We want you to bring the twins and Katie and visit us reg'lar. And we'll be callin' on you, too!"

"We'd been countin' on doin' just that," he admitted. "The little girls are plumb attached to their big brother."

With a polite nod to Lizzie, Alton moved past her until he was standing in front of Jem. "Well, son, I'm wishin' the two o' you all the happiness your mama and I knowed . . ." The big man fell silent as the emotion of the moment collided with his bittersweet memories.

"Thanks, Pa."

Alton cleared his throat. "Now, if you'll hold Marissa, I have somethin' for you." Fishing in his vest pocket, he produced a folded slip of parchment and handed it to Jem, then took the baby back. "It's to aid you in gettin' started on your own. From me and the three little girls."

Jem looked confused.

"Thanks, Pa, but you didn't have to get us anything," he said as he accepted the slip of paper. He drew Lizzie to him and gave her a quick hug, the note as yet unread. "We have everything we need."

"I know, son, I know," Alton said, his voice rough. "Didn't *have* to. *Wanted* to."

Jeremiah carefully unfolded the stiff paper, moving his lips as he read silently while Lizzie peered over his shoulder. When he came to the end, there was no containing Jem's grin. He gave a whoop of delight.

"Jeremiah Stone, what is it?" she demanded. "You know I can't see it!"

"*Mules, Liz!*" He stared at the bill of sale. "A pair of mules—"

"The best durn pair of jennies money could buy, Jem."

"Oh, Pa, thanks! Pa, you don't know what this means to us!"

Alton adjusted his fedora and riffled his dark hair. "Oh, I reckon I do at that," he said, obviously pleased that his gift had been so well received. "They'll mean to you about what ol' Doc and Dan have meant to me."

"Doc and Dan are fine horses," Jeremiah began. "In fact, they're the best draft horses in these parts, but—"

"But you've always been partial to workin' mules," Alton finished the thought for him. "Well, now you'll have your own team to assist you in sod bustin', boy. Though if you've a

8

need for my horses, you have only to give the word and they're yours to use."

"We can't thank you enough, Pa," Jeremiah said, shaking his head, touched by the gift, dazed with the joy of ownership.

Alton got down to business as Katie fussed and one of the babies squirmed against him. "The skinner promised he'd deliver the mules the day after tomorry. We allowed as how that'd give you some time to settle down a bit and prepare a stout pasture for the mules. But I'll drop by to make sure he keeps his word."

Jeremiah shook his pa's hand. "We'll look forward to seein' you then." His tone was both respectful and assertive, befitting his new role as head of his own household—a household that had increased by one wife and four stepchildren in the span of a single afternoon.

"Oh, but you're welcome *any* time, Pa Wheeler," Lizzie spoke up. "Don't wait for a special invite."

Alton smiled. "Now I'd best be gettin' these young'uns home." He moved aside to make way for other well-wishers who wanted to say their farewells.

With a large hand, he cupped a small head against his leg and encouraged Katie to keep up with him. After the long afternoon, the little girl was staggering with fatigue. And the twins, only a few winks away from sleep themselves, stirred fretfully in his arms.

"Jem, carry one of the girls to the wagon for your pa," Lizzie ordered. "He's got his hands plumb full."

Jeremiah scooped up a feisty Marissa, leaving the more placid Molly for Alton to deal with. Then he took Katie's hand to guide her around to the far side, helped tuck the girls in, then stepped back as his stepfather climbed into the springseat of the aging wagon.

"Thanks for comin', Pa," Jem said.

"Why, we wouldn't have missed seein' you 'n' Miss Lizzie joined in holy matrimony for nothin' in the world."

"Hurry back!" they called as Alton slapped the worn leather reins across the Clydesdales' broad backs, and the sleek team set out at a brisk trot.

With their arms about each other, the newlyweds bade farewell to the last of their guests and watched Alton and the girls as they jounced down the rutted road.

"Poor Pa Wheeler," Lizzie murmured under her breath. "Jem, did his shoulders droop just a little as he drove off? Or was it just my imaginin's?" She searched her new husband's face.

He gave a heavy sigh. "No, I saw it too. Pa seemed . . . sad. Real sad."

Lizzie's eyes grew luminous with compassion, and she bit her lip as the lonely little family was lost to view around a bend in the road. She gave a helpless sigh that matched her husband's.

"He's missin' you already, Jem. We'll have them over for dinner real often 'n' real soon," she planned aloud.

"I'd like that. Pa's going to need it. The girls, too."

"Without you there, he's goin' to be lonely—," Lizzie worried, "like I was after Harmon got killed . . . 'til you started comin' by to help me pass the time 'n' lend a hand with the young'uns 'n' make me remember what it was to laugh again . . . love again—"

Jeremiah gave Lizzie a hug which grew into a warm embrace when she leaned her head against his shoulder. Matching their steps, they followed the stone path leading to the cabin where the Prestons were tending to Lizzie's brood.

Her mood mellow, she was in no hurry to go inside.

"I sure do wish your pa'd find someone nice to marry so's

he could be as happy as he was with your mama . . . as happy as we are now—"

"Doesn't seem likely." Jem shook his head. "It would take a very special woman to fill Ma's place in Pa's heart."

Lizzie grew reflective. Then she turned to Jem in a gesture of frustration.

"For the life of me, Jeremiah, you're right. I can't think of a single woman of my acquaintance who's suitable for your pa to court." Her brow dipped to a frown before it was just as quickly eased in a smile. "But *Mama* may know someone. She knows just 'bout ever'body in these parts. If some of us gals set our minds to it, why we could have your pa hitched up in no time a'tall."

"Oh, Lizzie, Lizzie—" Jem smiled with amusement as he smoothed her hair from her face. "Don't count on it. For one thing, Pa won't cooperate. Alton Wheeler won't go looking for love. And you know as well as I that he'll turn tail and run from any woman who appears intent on snaring him. No, I'm afraid that love will have to sneak up and catch Pa unawares."

"That may be so," she concluded as she mulled over Jem's argument. "Not only will it have to sneak up on him, but bushwhack him in the bargain! Even so . . . it might not hurt to help things along a little. If Alton Wheeler won't go lookin' for a new love, then we'll just have to bring love to him!"

As if eager to change the subject, Jem leaned close and spoke in her ear. "Now are we going to go in the house, darlin', or are we going to stand here all night with the door open while you play matchmaker?"

"Maybe we just will!" Lizzie retorted with a wink. Moving forward purposefully, she just as quickly retraced her steps to him. "Carry me over the threshold, Jem?" she invited, suddenly shy. "Just like for a real bride . . . in a penny dreadful novel."

Despite the lilt in her voice, in her eyes he could read the hunger of a heart well acquainted with sorrow and suffering but too long denied love's tenderness.

Gallantly Jem swept Lizzie off her feet. Balancing his new bride in his arms, he braced the screen door with his back, booted the wooden door the rest of the way open, and staggered into the room with his giggling load intact.

"Whew, Lizzie! For a slip of a thing, you're plumb weighty. There you go," he said breathlessly, depositing her on the plank floor just inside the cabin door.

With a cautious glance toward the kitchen, Lizzie tightened her hold on him, smiling impishly into his eyes. Then her own eyes closed in anticipation as their lips met and lingered for the first time since her impulsive kiss at the altar.

"Mmmmm. *Nice,*" she purred, content.

Chancing another stolen kiss, Jem's arms moved around her once more. But the young couple drew quickly apart when Lizzie's sons spilled into the room with their grandmother on their heels, and Fanchon Preston crossed in front of them to lay the baby down in the cradle.

"Thad Childers! Put that cookie away!" Lizzie cried. "As much food as you've packed in today, you're goin' to be sick as a hound dog if you don't stop right now!"

"Oh . . . Ma—," Thad protested.

Jem noticed his hesitation, the moment of testing. Nor did he miss the boy's glance, cast in his direction, as if Thad were hopeful that his new stepfather would intervene on his behalf.

"Do as your mother says." Jeremiah quietly affirmed her stand.

Thad sighed and returned to the kitchen to replace the cookie in the crockery jar.

"We'd best be headin' for home," Fanny said, fetching her wrap and rousing Will from his warm place by the fire.

"Thanks for everythin', Mama," Lizzie whispered as the two women hugged.

Strolling with the Prestons to the front of the house, where their buggy was hitched to Will's sorrel mare, it was clear to Lizzie and Jem that her pa's rheumatiz was acting up again. He moaned with every step, and it took all of them to help him into the driver's seat beside Fanny. But he managed a smile as they turned toward home with a wave and a promise to "come again soon."

Minutes later, Jem and the boys stepped outside to attend to farm chores that could wait no longer, wedding or no wedding. And by the time they returned to the cozy cabin, Lizzie had a kettle of potato soup simmering on the large wood range.

"A light meal seemed in order after such a feast," she said as the family seated themselves around the oak dining table.

Lizzie ladled a rich soup from the tureen. While the others spooned their bowls empty, Thad made little progress in lowering the level in his bowl.

"Looks like Thad spoiled his appetite eating too many sweetmeats and treats today," Jem said, giving Lizzie's youngest son a fond look.

"Looks that way," she agreed, and reluctantly excused Thad from the table, along with Lester and Maylon, after deciding he'd dawdled over his supper long enough.

Beneath the table, Jem took Lizzie's hand. In silence, they watched the boys retreat to the adjacent room in the cabin.

"Thad seems a mite withdrawn, don't you think, Jem?"

He shrugged. "No more than Les and Maylon. This has been a big day for all of them."

"It's to be expected, I s'pose," Lizzie said with a sigh. "We've all been through a lot . . . for a long spell. Sometimes, when I think of what we've had to withstand, I almost feel like faintin' away from the weight of it all. An' it's downright scary to consider what we might still be asked to bear without bucklin' in the future, Jem." There was a faraway look in her eyes. "But when Harmon died, I found myself havin' to go on even though a part of me felt like it had died along with him—"

In the other room could be heard the sound of children talking, laughing. Lizzie spoke on. "Grief . . . it fades in the light of a strong faith, y'know . . . just like a chambray shirt fades out 'neath the sun's hot glare as it hangs on the line."

"Folks aren't shirts, Lizzie," Jem interrupted, trying to tease her out of her serious mood.

"I know that." She tossed her head, not easily dissuaded from voicing the thoughts that crowded her mind. "But it's a lot the same . . . leastways, as I see it. As happy as I am right now, Jeremiah Stone, I ain't foolish enough to b'lieve it'll last for always, 'cause barrin' a basketful of miracles, it can't. When Harm died, I'd have took on worse'n I did, 'cept I knowed we'd be together again up yonder. An' I'd start sheddin' tears now for Ma and Pa, 'cause they're gettin' on up in years, 'cept I realize that this life ain't but one little heartbeat when you stack it up against all the time of eternity. Am I makin' sense, Jeremiah?" she asked fervently, turning to study his face. "Or do you think I'm plumb crazy?"

She was surprised to see that his eyes were misty. "I think you're wise beyond your years, my darlin', and I know it was a loving and generous God who gave you to me. Someday, just like the Good Book says, your children will rise up and call you blessed—"

"Shush, now," she scolded, embarrassed. "I know you're goin' to be a dandy husband, and while it might tax your patience some, you're goin' to make a fine pa for my young'uns. But much as they all love you, Jem, lookin' on you as their pa will take some gettin' used to."

Jeremiah was a long moment framing a response. His thoughts flew back to the spring night when Alton Wheeler had taken his own dear mama for his bride, she a widow in mourning for a little more than a year. Jem, too, had mourned the passing of Nathan Stone, who had died in a mining accident on the Mesabi Iron Range in Northern Minnesota.

And that night, when Alton actually came to live with them, Jem had battled his own emotions. For no matter how much he'd come to love and respect Alton Wheeler, he couldn't believe that the big man would ever take his real pa's place. Now Harmon Childers's young'uns would have to make peace with his own presence in their lives, in their home.

"I won't intrude, nor try to force the issue," Jeremiah promised. "We'll proceed at the boys' pace. They know I'm their friend. In God's own time, maybe they'll view me as their pa, too."

"You're so wise, Jem," Lizzie said softly, her voice choked with emotion.

He laughed, intent on bringing some levity to the solemn discussion before reflections on the past could dampen the first night of their life together.

"So are *you,* woman, for falling in love with such a wise man. Aren't you proud of yourself for managing it?"

"'Course I am!" Lizzie bantered back.

"And didn't I know it! Why, if I hadn't proposed to you, no doubt you'd have asked Mama Fanchon to dig up her best-kept secrets!"

"Maybe I just would've at that!" Lizzie declared, blushing, her cheeks growing an even deeper rose when Jeremiah threw back his head and laughed.

Still sitting close, he stroked her cheek with his fingertip, murmuring words of endearment. She laid her head against the flat of his hand, her features hazy and soft with content.

"I think I'm just learnin' what love means," Lizzie whispered, her heart quickening, thinking of the time just ahead when they would be alone at last.

Before they could retire to the privacy of their own room, though, there were chores to do. Lizzie would do up the supper dishes, while Jem helped ready the boys for bed and banked the fire in the hearth. But now there were two to share the load.

The evening hours began like so many others after Harm Childers's passing. Harm hadn't lasted long, Jem recalled, after that log had fallen on him in the timber. Lizzie's heart had been broken, and very nearly her own will to live. It had taken all her friends and family to console her in her grief, to help her find the silver lining among the dark clouds that threatened to overshadow her. Lizzie—with the fiery temper, the quick wit, the laughing face—had almost ceased to exist for a time, until Jem fanned the spark that had never been quite extinguished, and brought her back.

The hours crept by, or so it seemed to Jem, who could not help pondering the enormity of the husbandly duty that lay before him. As he played checkers with the boys, taking turns against each of them, Jem watched his new wife in the lamplight, doing the homey little things that women do. And later, after the boys had gone up the ladder to the loft, they sat on the horsehair sofa as baby Harmony dozed in the maple cradle, talking quietly, dreaming, awed in the knowledge that no longer would the hour come for Jem to strike out for a home apart from the one he shared with Lizzie.

When the grandfather clock bonged nine times, Lizzie yawned, caressed Jem's shoulder, and reached up to take the coal oil lamp from the mantel where it had cast its light on the snug room.

Hesitantly, a bit uncertain, Jem arose to accompany her. Quietly they crossed to the dim bedroom. Lizzie set the lamp on a shelf above the bed, its mattress supported by stout ropes. Shadows danced on the chinked, rough-hewn walls.

To Jem's dismay, instead of remaining there with him, Lizzie lit a candle and, shielding the flame with her hand, turned to leave.

"I'll only be a jiffy, Jeremiah. I'm goin' to check on the young'uns one last time . . . so we won't be . . . disturbed. Thad *did* seem peaked at supper. I sure do hope he's not comin' down with somethin'."

"Too many sweets," he said again.

"Maybe. Maybe not. There's been some sickness goin' 'round—"

When Lizzie departed, Jem welcomed the privacy to prepare himself for bed. So he had shed his clothing and was snugged beneath the thick quilts when she returned.

Fascinated, Jem watched her quick movements, memorizing her ritual. With crisp gestures—somehow more seductive than the bawdiest displays at the burlesque shows he'd witnessed during the rebellious days following his mother's passing—Jem watched Lizzie loosen her prim clothing. Unpinning her hair, she shook her head, and the glossy chestnut tresses flung free.

Sitting down on the crackling tick beside him, she picked up a boar brush and began dragging the bristles through her hair until the locks were smooth and tangle-free, floating like a silk cloud about her shoulders.

Unable to take his eyes off her, Jem caught the sweet rain-washed scent and reached to touch a single strand.

"So beautiful . . . you're so beautiful, Liz."

Boosting himself on an elbow, he regarded her in the dim glow of the lamp. And before she knew it, Jem had doused the light and pulled her into his arms.

Suddenly, without warning, Lizzie sprang from him, leaving Jem's arms achingly empty. Clutching her gown to her dress, with its slipping basque, she whirled to confront the doorway of their room, and strained to discern the source of the noise that had caught her attention.

"It's nothing," Jem said, listening, but being rewarded with nothing but silence.

Then, just outside the curtain that hung in the doorway of their room, a board creaked.

"Who is it?" Lizzie called out.

She boosted herself from the bed, setting her feet to the cold floor as she went to investigate, doing up her dress as she did.

"Mama—" came a whimper. "I don't feel so good—"

"It's Thad!"

Lizzie fumbled her way to the door, while Jem groped for matches and managed to light the lamp. When he replaced the globe, it magnified the flame that danced on the wick dangling into the reservoir of golden kerosene in the lamp's base.

"Thad's feverish," said Lizzie, laying a hand across his forehead.

"Too much celebrating."

"No." Lizzie was certain it was more. She flicked back the coverlets and prepared a place in the bed to nest the sick child. "I'll tuck you in between Jem 'n' me so's I can keep an eye on you, honey."

"All right, Mama."

The child crawled onto the tick and snuggled down beside

Jem. Giving his new pa a weak smile, he slowly closed his eyes.

At Harmony's fretful cry, Lizzie jerked her cotton night-dress and wrapper from the nail pounded in the wall near the chifforobe and fled the room to comfort her. And when, much later, she returned, she was wearing her modest cotton nightgown.

The coal oil lamp burned low. Thad was fast asleep. His lower lip puffed in and out with every labored breath.

Lizzie's eyes sought Jem's in an unspoken apology. He gave her a soft smile.

"Poor little tyke's pretty sick, I can see that," he observed. "What's ailing him is no bellyache from too many sweets, either."

"I know," Lizzie murmured with a frown. She placed her palm against Thad's forehead—hot to her touch. His cheeks were brick red. "He's sick all right, Jem. I can feel the fever." She sniffed. "Can smell it, too. I'd best fetch a cool compress for his forehead."

Lizzie left the room, returning with a wet cloth that she applied to Thad's brow. At the contact, the child moaned in pain. Then, as his skin drew the chill from the rag, he sank back into restless slumber.

Knowing that they could do no more for him at the moment, Lizzie reached over to turn down the lamp, looking toward Jem with a sad, regretful smile.

With his arm around young Thad, Jem's hand touched Lizzie's. Gratefully she accepted his strong grip, her heart swelling. To her, this masculine hand, so rough and work-scarred, had never seemed so beautiful as when he'd reached for her in an adoring expression of his unconsummated love.

"I'm sorry, Jeremiah, that our weddin' night will have to wait," Lizzie whispered into the darkness.

"The children's needs come first, darlin'. I know that. I can bear another night of postponement. . . ." Jem paused, feeling Thad's hot brow. "Or even *many* nights, if need be."

As he turned over on his side, she heard his long sigh of quiet acceptance. "Besides, we have the rest of our lives. . . ."

chapter
2

AT DAWN Lizzie's eyes flicked open and fell on her sleeping child, sheltered by Jeremiah's strong body. Thad slept with the restlessness of one consumed with fever.

She slid from bed, reaching for her robe. Hastily she tiptoed across the wood floor, her teeth chattering with the drafty chill. Pulling her faded wrapper around her, she knelt before the hearth and grabbed a poker, stirring the ashes as she raked the glowing coals into a pile.

Lizzie filled the graniteware pot with water, measured out coffee beans, spun the crank of the grinder, and emptied the small drawer that caught the grounds. It clanked when she tapped it smartly against the rim of the pot, and the fine dark grains floated on the water drawn from the cistern the evening before.

Then she hung the pot on the iron rod and swung it into place over the fire as the flames danced higher.

Lizzie wasn't sure how many times Thad had called to her before his croaky voice registered, and she rushed to him.

"Shush, honey," she said, entering the cozy bedroom. "Let Jem sleep."

"I don't feel good."

"Tell Mama what's wrong."

21

Lizzie scooped the lad into her arms and transferred him to a hastily constructed pallet near the hearth. Here the fire roared comfortingly and sent heat rushing out into the room where Harmony slept in her cradle.

"My head hurts . . . 'n' I'm cold," Thad admitted in a small voice. "When I try to lift my head . . . I feel all sick 'n' dizzy."

"You'll feel better in a day or two. Sure hope it ain't somethin' catchy, though, 'specially with Harmony so little." She smoothed his cowlick. "You try to sleep now, honey. Rest's the best medicine in the world."

"I feel sleepy . . . but kinda hungry, too."

"Anythin' special you'd like this mornin', Thad? Somethin' that appeals to you as puny as you're feelin'?"

"Johnny cake . . . with butter . . . 'n' lots of syrup."

"I'll bake it so's the crust is golden 'n' crispy—just the way you like it."

By the time Lizzie had breakfast on, Harmony was ready to arise for the day.

"Boys!" Lizzie called out, shaking the attic ladder for emphasis. "Time to get up! Breakfast's 'bout ready to set on the table. Hurry now! They's chores to do."

A moment later the sleepy-eyed boys climbed down, proceeded to the kitchen, and sloshed noisily in the basin of warm water on the washstand.

"What's wrong with Thad?" Lester asked.

"He's feelin' kind of puny today."

"Too many cookies yesterday?"

"I don't think so, but I'm not sure," Lizzie said, trying to suppress the worry she felt. "Prob'ly just the gallopin' miseries. I'll ask Ma . . . she'll know what to do. Besides, he'll be fine in a day or two."

But he wasn't.

By evening, Thad's malaise increased.

The next day he was even worse.

Finally, on the third day, when his jaws began to swell, the diagnosis was clear.

"Mumps—," Lizzie sighed the dread verdict, then groaned.

Fanny seemed unconcerned.

"Almost no one dies of mumps, child. They just bring discomfort. No, it's *growed* men who have cause to worry. Why, when the illness migrates in their bodies, they can sometimes suffer damage—" Fanny's expression changed to one of grim horror. "—damage that stays with 'em for life!"

"But what'll we do for *Thad,* Ma?" persisted a preoccupied Lizzie, getting to the business at hand.

Fanny gave a helpless gesture. "Let nature run her course. Give 'im plenty of bed rest and good food, 'long with hot or cold packs on his jaws to afford him a bit of comfort."

"That's all?" Dismay was evident in Lizzie's tone.

Fanchon shrugged. "Not much else to do but watch 'im and wait."

"And *worry*."

In the next few days, as often as he could leave his chores, Jem was at Thad's side, nursing the sick child to give Lizzie a brief respite or to allow her to tend the baby or prepare a meal.

"Do you think we'd better send for the doctor, Liz?" he asked one day when all their efforts to bring down Thad's temperature had failed.

"He's still got a powerfully high fever."

"I know. Mama said to expect it. But if it don't break by mornin', Jem, then you can fetch the doctor."

But by the next morning, Thad seemed better.

It was Maylon and Lester who were unusually quiet. "Will we get the mumps, Ma?" they asked.

"I don't rightly know, boys," Lizzie replied. "Grandma says

23

they ain't near as catchy as the measles. And, it takes long enough to catch 'em that, unless you were exposed along with Thad, you'll be awhile comin' down with 'em."

"What about you, Ma, 'n' Harmony?"

"Gran says your Uncle Rory, he was so swole up with parotitis that he looked like the man in the moon! An' I recollect havin' the mumps once, leastways on one side. You ain't s'posed to be able to catch 'em twice—though I've heard tell there's rare folks as does. I expect I'm too ornery to catch 'em again, though," she assured the boys. "As for Harmony . . . wee babes don't usually come down with such serious illnesses. Even so, we'll have to remember to ask the Lord to keep our little sweetheart safe."

"What about Jeremiah?" Maylon persisted.

Lizzie dried her hands on a faded dishtowel. "I don't know for certain, and neither does Jem. Jem's a growed man. Like as not, he had the mumps when he was comin' up in northern Minnesota, where he and his mama lived before the Stones moved to these parts 'n' she married Alton."

But Jeremiah had not had the mumps.

Alton recalled how Sue Ellen had worried about him during the last siege of parotitis that had run through the neighborhood, seeming to strike victims in a whimsical pattern, ignoring some while incapacitating others in the same household.

Fourteen days went by.

Then twenty-one.

Midway through the fourth week, Jem complained of chills. When Lizzie murmured about mumps, he shrugged it off and laid blame to the light spring rain—misery to work in, but heaven-sent for the pastures that were already greening up.

"You'd best take care of yourself, Jem," Lizzie cautioned.

24

"I will, Liz. Just as soon as I take care of the mules and slop the hogs and collect the eggs—"

She rolled her eyes and waved him out the door. The sooner he got to work, the sooner he'd be done.

Jem seemed to hurry through the chores, Lizzie thought, because he had them done, and a supply of wood hauled in, neatly stacked in the wood box beside the range almost before the boys abandoned their horseplay in time to help.

Since Lizzie kept up a steady stream of chatter after he came in, it was almost bedtime before she realized that Jeremiah sounded hoarse. Then she recalled how he'd winced when he'd taken a sip of hot coffee—as if it hurt to swallow.

When she hugged Jem and kissed him goodnight, she accused him of being feverish, but he laughed it off, complimenting her on the quality of the quilts she made that could keep a body so warm.

The next day Jem was up at dawn, as was Lizzie. The household was in a stir, with the activity increasing when Alton and the Wheeler girls arrived in late afternoon.

Alton, who'd been to town that day, stopped by and dispensed penny candy sticks to the children, along with area gossip for Lizzie and Jem. Soon he began to talk about leaving.

"You can't head home already, Pa Wheeler," cried Lizzie. "Seems you just got here. Stay to dinner with us, 'n' I'm warnin' you, I won't take no for an answer—not when I'm fully satisfied that you've no supper waitin' for you at home."

"That I don't, Lizzie-girl," Alton admitted.

"May as well stay, Pa. Lizzie's made up her mind," Jem explained, grinning proudly. "What do you say we vacate the kitchen? Though the heat from the stove is mighty appealing,

25

Liz will be creating whirlwinds as she puts the vittles on the table."

"You don't have to leave," Lizzie protested, even as she welcomed free run of the room.

"I wanted to show Pa how well the mules are doing."

Lizzie rolled her eyes. "Mules!" she exploded theatrically, giving Jem an exasperated look. "I never woulda thought it, Pa Wheeler. The sweet words Jem used to bestow on me afore we were married, he now saves for his prize mules!"

"Such a pity," Alton commiserated.

"I dasn't even tell you how much he adores those long-eared, runt-tailed, raucous beasts."

"That I do, Pa," Jem admitted with a grin. "I reckon I'm fond of Birdie and Mavis because those two jennies remind me of Liz."

"Well, I do declare!" Lizzie huffed.

"Not in looks, mind you," Jem quickly clarified. "But they're every bit her equal when it comes to stubbornness."

"And don't forget the ability to work hard 'n' long," Alton chimed in.

"Equal in stubbornness?" Lizzie challenged, ignoring her father-in-law's attempt at diplomacy. "You'll be out in the barn with your cherished mules if you keep up that kind of talk, my dear husband!"

Jem's contented laugh rang through the air as he and Alton stepped outside. But away from the warm kitchen, he was helpless to contain the chills and the waves of heat that, by turn, wracked his body.

Alton stared at him. "You ain't feelin' too fit, are you, son?"

"Not too pert," he admitted. "Reckon it's a cold coming on. Spring colds are always the worst."

"Hope that's all 'tis," Alton murmured. "You recollect, don't ya, that the mumps has been goin' around?"

26

Jem shrugged. "Fanny said a person will generally come down with the mumps within three weeks after exposure. It's better than four now."

"There's an exception to ever' rule, son. When I was a whippersnapper, a young feller on a neighborin' farm took 'em long after ever'one else was over 'em."

"I'll be all right," Jem said, as if sheer determination would make it true. "Liz has her hands full enough with one sick young'un and tending Harmony too. I'll tough it out."

"Then you'd best take care of yourself," Alton warned, "just like Lizzie's been urgin' you to do. Let Lester 'n' Maylon do the chores for a day or two."

Jem shook his head. "Young as they are, I hesitate laying my work on them. Surely all I've got is a head cold that can't decide where to settle."

Alton unlatched the gate and Jem passed through, stopping to gaze lovingly at the mules, who ambled over at his approach.

When they nosed his hand, he ran his fingers through their coats that were shedding in balled-up tufts in response to balmy warm breezes. Enjoying the caresses, the mules rippled their hides, flicked their long ears, and brayed noisily.

"They're prime stock," Jem said. "And good mules bring a good price."

"That they do. But worth it too. It almost pains me to admit it," Alton said and gave a rueful chuckle, "but mules can do things horses can't."

"Yeah, like *think*," Jem reminded him, grinning. "A horse will work itself to death, but not a mule. When that critter's tired, he's smart enough to lie down and refuse to take another step."

"Overwork will never kill a mule," Alton agreed, "but many a mule skinner'll threaten to."

27

"Aw, you've just got to know how to work 'em."

"Well, you have the knack and the patience, too, I'll grant you that."

"I've been giving it some thought, Pa," Jem went on. "And I'd kind of like to go into the mule-raising business, help out with cash in addition to crops. With four young'uns now, and maybe more—if the Lord sees fit to bless us—selling mules could go a long way toward meeting expenses . . . and give me a little change to buy a few fancies for Liz. She does work so hard—"

Alton listened as Jem spun his dreams. Then he gave the boy an affectionate clap on the shoulder and turned him toward the house when he noticed that Jem was in the grip of another chill.

"Dandy plans, son. But it'll take good health to carry 'em out. You need to start right now—by hying yourself into that cabin where it's warm. An' it ain't selfish to take a bit more rest for yourself—"

"I will," Jem agreed, waving off his concern. "Starting tomorrow."

But by then it was too late.

By midnight, Jem's fever had risen.

By sunup, his throat had constricted so that he could scarcely swallow. The glands in his cheeks ballooned.

Clucking in sympathy, Lizzie bustled around the cabin, stealing minutes from her workday to minister to Jeremiah's needs. But more and more often, his low moans and restless thrashing summoned her to his side.

Lizzie kept him warm, spooned broth between his shaking lips, and applied soothing compresses to his cheeks, tying the muslin strips in place with a carefully folded towel. Her efforts relieved the discomfort, but did not bring a cure.

Seven days later, still weak but stubbornly resolved, Jem left his sickbed, announcing his plans to resume the barnyard chores the boys had performed in his stead.

"It's too soon, Jem," Lizzie pleaded. "I'm afraid you'll overdo. The boys don't mind helpin' out more. Truly they don't! No one thinks you're shirkin' your duties."

But nothing anyone could say convinced him.

Just as Fanny had feared, Jem was soon back in bed, his groin swollen until the slightest movement caused him agony. Faced with her husband's suffering, Lizzie blinked back tears and swallowed the words, *I told you so!*

But it was at least a month before Jem had begun to gain back his strength. Still absent was the weight he'd quickly dropped, a loss his lean frame could ill afford.

"He'll be bouncin' back fast now," Fanny assured Lizzie. "Just fix Jeremiah hearty meals 'n' feed him often. He'll soon be . . . ahem—" She cleared her throat pointedly, and dropped her voice to a discreet whisper. "—almost as good as new again."

Fanny frowned thoughtfully and paused over the needlework in her lap as if she were about to say more, but Lizzie was already talking excitedly about plans for the Watson Fair that was scheduled to take place in the upcoming warm months.

"I'll be doin' lots of bakin' and preserve-makin' to enter in the open competition this year, Mama." Then, catching sight of the portrait on the mantel, she spoke reflectively. "I'm so thankful I've got that picture of Harmon 'n' me. An' I'm wantin' to get some more pictures took, too—not just of Jem, me, and the young'uns, but of you, Pa, and Rory, and Alton and the little girls, iffen they'll sit still long enough!"

"Lizzie, Lizzie!" Fanny said, laughing at the silly notion. "Jeremiah would give you the moon and stars if you asked for 'em, but you can't be demandin' fancies, sweetheart, when there's things he needs for the farm."

Lizzie tossed her long hair and thrust out her chin. "I ain't askin' Jem for the money, Mama. I—I'm goin' to get the money for the pictures myself."

"Now, just how do you plan to do that?" Fanny asked in surprise, knowing there were very few jobs for decent women.

"I've already told you. I'm goin' to bake and cook up a storm. I'll enter somethin' in ever' competition at the Watson Fair. And I'll save up my premium money. And in addition, I'm a-goin' to enter the contests on the midway—the nail-drivin' competition, the hog-callin' contest, the greased-pig catchin' contest—"

As Lizzie rattled off her litany of intentions, Fanny began to chuckle again.

"And just what do you find so all-fired funny, Mama?" Lizzie asked, wounded.

"Nothin', darlin'." Fanny wiped the dampness from the corners of her eyes. "I was jus' thinkin' of you tryin' to catch a greased pig, is all!"

Lizzie gave a weak laugh. "Well, guess you won't think it's so funny when we march into the photographer's, spiffed up purty as you please in our Sunday-go-to-meetin' clothes," she sniffed. "I'm not only goin' to get Jeremiah and me a nice big picture of all o' us, but one for you 'n' Pa, too, iffen I can afford it."

"We don't need no picture, honey."

But Lizzie's chin was set. "I've got my heart set on it, Mama. So don't think to change my mind."

Fanny only shook her head helplessly. "Dear me, you *are* as stubborn as Jeremiah's mules!"

"Jem's a caution over them mules, ain't he, Mama?" Lizzie said, glad to change the subject. "He's bound and determined to be well enough to hitch up Birdie and Mavis to begin workin' the field just as soon as it's dry enough," Lizzie said. "Fact is, I've been wishin' he'd hie himself on out to the field so's I can practice. We've got a sow with a litter of nice-sized shoats. I figger to pen her up, turn those little porkers loose, and practice catchin' pigs so that I'll be a shoo-in for first prize come Watson Fair time!"

"Then you're serious 'bout your picture-takin' notions, ain't you?"

"Serious as the pox!" Lizzie insisted, giving a curt nod. "If I'm to practice catchin' those shoats, I figger a muddy piglet ought to be nigh on 'bout as slippery as a greased one."

"Well, good luck to ya," said Fanny, "but you be careful. A riled up ol' sow's somethin' to reckon with. Oh, well, afore you know it, summer'll be here, and the swill'll be dried up . . . fields, too."

Lizzie looked worried. "Jeremiah's been complainin' 'bout all the rain that's kept him outa the fields. About the time it gets dry enough to plow, along comes another little shower and muddies things up again."

Fanny sniffed. "He's right. Better to work the fields too dry than to plow when it's downright wet. Fight mudballs 'til harvest, then."

"Jem's anxious. What farmer isn't? You've heard the menfolk talk."

Fanny nodded. "This's the first spring that Will Preston hasn't been chompin' at the bit to sink a plow into the good earth. But Rory's rarin' to hitch the team and get goin', stump-leg and all."

"Rory's doin' well with his peg leg, is he?" Lizzie asked, feeling a wave of relief cascade over her. Sometimes her younger brother could be as changeable as a pellet of mercury.

"Whittled himself a right workable one. Even joshed about

31

what wood to use. Said that cottonwood would warp on 'im if he walked through mud, that hickory'd attract squirrels—"

"Praise God that Rory's accepted his lot, Mama, and is able to joke about the misfortune that's befallen him."

"I'm not sure he *has* accepted it, Lizzie."

"What do you mean, Mama? Why, the way he's always smilin', cuttin' up, makin' jokes—"

"Sometimes folks laugh to keep from cryin', y' know."

"There've been signs of maturin' in Rory, though, Mama. I know he's expectin' to be a big help to Pa this year."

"And I thank the good Lord for that. Pa's tired, Lizzie . . . tireder'n I've ever seen 'im. Reckon he's gettin' old . . . we both are—"

"Don't say that, Ma!" At her mother's words, Lizzie's heart gave a painful wrench.

Fanny paused mid-stitch, her eyes resting on her daughter before she turned her head to stare out over the meadow. When she finally spoke again, her voice was low and gentle.

"Pa's tired, Lizzie. That's the truth, girl . . . 'n' the truth's for speakin'. Your Pa's some older'n me, Lizzie, and I'm not a spring chick anymore, y' know. Our days are numbered, lambie . . . for both of us . . . for all of us—"

Lizzie abandoned her work. She faced her mother with desperate, searching eyes.

"Mama! Tell me true . . . Pa's not sick with the wastin' away disease, is he?"

"Oh, no, darlin'! I didn't mean to disturb you with my talk. After all, we're born to die 'n' leave this world for a better one. Pa's no doubt got a good many years left. He's just gettin' tired, is all. Needin' to slow down. I gather he's content to turn the fields over to Rory. Not only that," Fanchon confided, "but don't s'pose he'd mind my tellin' ya he's considerin' handin' his fiddle on down to your Jeremiah."

Lizzie gasped, speechless as the full meaning of her mother's words dawned.

"But Pa *loves* that fiddle, Mama. It's like a part of him—"

Fanny nodded. "That's right. An' a body only passes on his treasures to those who'll treasure 'em in turn. Rory never has put much stock in fiddle-playin'. He's always been too busy dancin'. It's Jem who'll set his own pleasure aside so's to make music for others."

Lizzie felt her eyes tingle with tears. Already she could see Jem stroking the bow of her pa's fiddle over the catgut strings, a distant smile on his face as the instrument tremulously issued forth its myriad sweet sounds.

"Jem will be so honored, Mama."

"But let's allow your pa to do the tellin'," Fanny suggested, feeling she might have spoken out of turn. "Just thought you'd treasure knowin' how much your papa approves of the man you've wed."

Lizzie smiled through a haze of tears. "Surely Pa knows that Jeremiah returns the feelin'. Why, Jem told me not long ago that when we have a young'un, iffen it's a boy child, he'll be named William, after Pa—"

Fanny halted her work to stare at Lizzie as if she couldn't believe her ears. Slowly, biding her time, she plucked lint from the fabric, picking her words just as carefully.

"You 'n' Jem pretty set on havin' more young'uns, are you?"

Lizzie nodded, blushing, but her eyes gleamed with a radiance reserved for moments spent reflecting on a cherished dream.

"Enough so's I'm goin' to wean Harmony onto a cup early, and have milk from the cow for her, in hopes of enlargin' our family that much sooner."

"Then my prayers will be that you can do just that," Fanny

said with simple forthrightness. But her countenance hinted that she scarcely dared hope that Lizzie's dreams would come true, though Lizzie seemed as determined to bear Jeremiah's baby as she was intent on walking away with every prize at the Watson Fair.

Lizzie knew that her cooking and baking skills could win top honors, hands down. But she was convinced that, despite her slim build, she could win some other contests, too. She was strong, could drive a spike as hard and as straight as a lot of men.

"I'd practice when no one's around," she muttered to herself, "iffen nails warn't so expensive." Sold by the pound, spikes were not something to be wasted, and Lizzie had straightened out enough bent nails in her lifetime not to relish the thought of repeating that task.

Well, pigs weren't that delicate! The first time she could hoodwink Jeremiah into taking the young'uns to town with him, she was going to slip into her old dress, shuck off her shoes, and practice capturing the husky little shoats who lazed around the murky swill!

Lizzie got her chance three days later, on a glorious, sunshiny morning freshened by a crisp, cool breeze. Jeremiah and the boys had plans to hitch the mules and drive by Pa Wheeler's before continuing on to town, while Mama had promised to look in on Harmony.

No sooner had the mules plodded out of the yard and onto the main trail than Lizzie whisked off her apron, her nimble fingers flying over buttons and snaps, and swapped her durable housedress for a frock that had long since been destined for the ragbag.

She kicked off her brogans, unrolled her stockings and put them up for safekeeping, and slipped outside.

The rock that served as a step at the back door was cool against her bare feet, and the ground was chilly and damp, but Lizzie plunged ahead, moving straight for the pig-lot like a ship under full sail.

She let herself into the lot. Just as she had hoped, the shoats, who could slide in and out under the fence slats, obliged her by darting out into the confines of the mule pasture from whence they turned to give her curious looks.

The sow, who had been lying in the shade of her pen, gave a contented grunt, flicked a fly off her ear, and closed her eyes as she returned to her slumber.

Trying not to frighten the pigs, Lizzie bounded around the pasture. In no time, she was short of breath, sweat dripping in her eyes. But the piglets, who at first had frisked about the pasture just out of reach, were becoming winded, too.

As Lizzie began to gain on a red and black spotted shoat, she tripped over a root. As it flung her ahead, she reached out, full length, and a grubby hand closed around a tiny little pork hock.

The piglet squealed with alarm, its cries high and shrill. Lizzie wallowed it toward her, wrestling it, wondering how a tiny creature who weighed only a fraction of what she did, could fight so valiantly.

She boosted herself to her feet, staggering beneath the weight of the squirming shoat, grimacing as she arched her neck back to remove her face from the pig's wildly twisting head.

"Gotcha!" she cried triumphantly.

She knew that the winner of the greased pig contest would have to carry the protesting porker all the way to the judge's stand, and she wasn't about to release the shoat until she was good-and-ready.

Lizzie was nearing the gate to the mule pasture—the

judge's stand, in her fantasy—when she heard boards splinter, and the angry "boof! boof!" of an enraged sow.

"Heavens to Betsy!" gasped Lizzie.

Ordinarily, Lulabelle, their prize sow, was a docile creature, but at that moment Lizzie recognized the fire in the aging pig's eyes. And, forgetting the piglet in her arms, she bolted toward the gate with Lulabelle in hot pursuit, her squalls and gnashing tusks punctuating Lizzie's sudden terror.

"Drop that pig, Lizzie!" Fanny bawled, having appeared as if from nowhere. "Drop that shoat, I say, afore that ol' sow rips you limb from gut!"

At her mama's words, Lizzie recalled the piglet in her arms and hastily dropped it, then proceeded to get entangled in her long skirts. She staggered ahead, pitching headlong, and tried to grasp a weatherbeaten fencepost as momentum sent her shooting by, but her palms were wet from the muddy piglet, and her grip failed.

"No!" she howled.

Lizzie tried to backstep but to no avail. Once her bare toes hit the damp clay ground surrounding the deep, murky swill, there was no stopping, and she skidded into the hog wallow, sending up a spray of muddy, stinking water.

Lizzie was weeping as she managed to catch her footing on the slick floor of the swill, wallowed out by an endless number of hogs who, through the years, had cooled off here in the muddy slop.

Rivers of filth ran down her as she stood like a clay statue, her eyes mere slits in the muddy ochre of her face.

"Mama! Help!" Lizzie bawled, retching from the odor.

"Hold still! I'm a-comin'!" Fanny called back. "Just keep your eyes closed! I'll get a stick for you to grab onto!"

Half an hour later, as Lizzie luxuriated in a quickly heated tub of water, Fanny returned from disposing of the muddy garments where no one would find them.

"Reckon we ought to shampoo your hair one last time?" Fanny asked. She leaned over to sniff Lizzie's damp locks. "Humph! Appears we'd better! One last time should do it. That, and a few drops of Lemon Verbena in the rinse water."

"Thanks, Mama," said Lizzie at last, toweling her long hair dry. "I don't know what I'd have done without you. But I don't think I'm gonna practice catchin' shoats again."

"Judgin' by what I've seen today, honey, you're a shoo-in. An' no girl can pound a nail as hard 'n' straight as you can. No one can outyell you, either. Why, all you'll have t'do is pretend you're stuck in a hog swill, and it'll inspire you to holler loud and long."

"Now don't tease me, Mama. I'm doin' this for all o' us!"

"I know y'are, darlin'," Fanny said, "and I've been thinkin' 'bout that fam'ly picture. I know you're wantin' to win the money at the fair, and I have full confidence you will. But if you happen to turn up a few dollars short, don't you worry, Lizzie-girl, 'cause your ol' mama's got a few coins put by, and I can't think of a nicer way to spend 'em than to have the smilin' faces of my dear ones right there on my mantel where I can look at 'em any time I choose!"

"Then we'll set up the appointment, Ma," Lizzie promised, "just as soon as the fair's over. And we won't take no for an answer. Pa and Jem and Rory can complain as much as they want 'bout missin' a day in the field. But first things first! And a fam'ly picture is the top order of the summer!"

chapter
3

"I DECLARE, I've never had so much fun in all my natural borned days!" said Fanny Preston, wiping tears of laughter from her cheeks as both Jeremiah and Will helped her into Jem's buckboard, hitched to a pair of mules that had won compliments from all of the farmers gathered at the Watson Town Fair.

"Fun for you, Mama," Lizzie said, giving a weary chuckle, "but 'twas sure enough hard work for me."

"Your pa and I taught you to labor well, child. You succeeded at everything you turned your hand to today, Lizzie-girl!"

"Wasn't she a caution?" Rory said. "Don't mind sayin' I was proud of you, Sis!"

"You just remember to smile for the photographer, Rory Preston, the way you've been smilin' all day long!"

"Is there goin' to be room up there for me?" asked Will, surveying the area where the youngsters sat crowded around the greased pig Lizzie had caught.

Jeremiah had deposited the animal into a tote sack, twining the lip of the bag closed, and now it awaited transportation to a pen Lizzie had waiting back at the farm.

"Sure is, Pa," Jem said. "I'll sit back here with the

young'uns and Lizzie's pig. You can drive the mules . . . that is, unless you'd rather give Lemont Gartner a hand, skinning that stubborn jack of his. I suspect he brought him to the fair in hopes of getting shed of the beast, but with the weather so dry and pastures turning brown, most folks are content to make do with what they've got."

Lemont's jenny mule was straining to pull ahead, but the jack had braced his legs, laid back his ears, and curled his lip into a sneer.

"Think we ought to give 'im a hand, Jem?" Rory asked, wincing as he tried to rise from the wagonbed, balancing his peg leg against a board to gain leverage.

"Yeah, I suppose—"

Jeremiah's response was cut short when the balky mule suddenly sprang ahead as if he'd been singed with a branding iron. Lemont's buckboard banged over the rutted fairground, the conveyance jouncing as his cousin from Philadelphia tried to hold on to both his hat and the wagon seat, apparently deciding that a lost bowler was preferable to a broken neck. Now he clung to the seat with a white-knuckled grip as the sweating jenny mule tried valiantly to keep up with the larger, stronger jack.

"Look at Lem's cousin!" Lizzie cried, grinning as she saw his coattails flapping in the breeze. "That's a ride that poor city feller won't soon forget!"

"Living with his country cousin for a few days while they get acquainted will sure be an experience for him," agreed Jem. "I'll wager it's different from anything he's ever done!"

"I can't remember the day I laughed this hard," Lizzie said, leaning her head on Jeremiah's shoulder. "I'm plumb tuckered out from laughin'."

Fanny looked back at Lizzie and her family, seated comfortably on the straw and enjoying the ride home. "Lord knows, you've known your share o' tears and heartaches. It's about time they was some good times to think back on."

"Sure do hope it lasts," Lizzie sighed.

"Weren't you the one telling me that nothing lasts forever?" Jem inquired, giving her a squeeze.

"I didn't mean for us to go gettin' serious, Jem. Not tonight. . . . Come tomorrow we can get back to the business of work and worry."

There were precious few moments after the fair to sit and dream, and what free moments there were that summer were spent discussing the education of the community's children.

"Thad's needing some schooling, Pa," Jem said one afternoon after chores. "He has a real quick mind and would do well with some instruction. I've taught him what I know, and he's eager for more."

Alton nodded. "It's right for our young'uns to be taught better'n most of us. I know a heap about a lotta things, but I ain't got no formal schoolin' like you 'n' your ma."

"Liz and I have talked with some folks. We're considering the idea of building our own school and hiring a schoolmarm, so our young'uns can stay home but still get a fine education."

"That's a dandy idea," Alton said. "No reason why we shouldn't."

"The plans are for the menfolk in the community to put up a log house for the school and a smaller one for the teacherage."

A meeting was called, and Alton was voted as one of the representatives to travel to Effingham in hopes of hiring a teacher to staff the newly constructed school. And within the month, the teacher, a young woman with pale golden hair and a sweet face, Miss Abigail Buckner, had been installed as the area's schoolmarm.

The older women viewed Miss Abby, an orphan, with maternal affection, while those nearer her age regarded her as fondly as a favorite sister.

Conscientious and hard-working, grateful not to have been passed over for someone with better qualifications for the teaching post, Miss Abby bloomed beneath the community's caring acceptance. She never lacked for invitations to dine with the parents and grandparents of the pupils she would instruct, and she became a regular participant in all community events, as one family or another was kind enough to attend to her travel necessities.

Fanny and Lizzie reserved plenty of dinner dates for Miss Abby to dine with them when she was free, and folks in the neighborhood thought it perfectly natural that Alton Wheeler and his three motherless girls were usually included in the invitation.

"It's worked out well, bringing Miss Abby into our midst, hasn't it, Pa?" asked Jem as they enjoyed coffee after polishing off a huge Sunday dinner.

"Sure has," Alton agreed, but said no more.

He had been quite close-mouthed about the selection process, except to relay to the area residents that the only male applicant had been kind of a "weak sister" who might have discipline problems, while the other likely candidate had been a "stern old crow."

"That settled it for me," Alton had said when he returned from Effingham. "Miss Abby was the right person for the job."

No mention was made of her obvious physical attributes, however, and eventually the womenfolk began to murmur among themselves that the fact might actually be lost on Alton Wheeler. So true was he to his departed wife's memory that he appeared oblivious to other women—even the pretty young schoolmarm who was being regularly thrown right under his nose.

"Miss Abby fits into the area like a hand into a glove," Lizzie said some months after the schoolteacher's arrival when she was settled into the teacherage and had begun her duties. "An', Rory Preston—" She fixed her brother with a knowing gaze. "—may I point out that Abigail Buckner is more than a little pleasin' to the eye? Or hadn't you noticed?"

Rory wasn't given a chance to respond, for Jem broke out in a loud guffaw.

"No doubt that was one of the first things Pa noticed about her, wouldn't you say?"

A startled Alton gave an indignant gasp. "Why, you cheeky young pup! I never! As I've told you afore, it boiled down to a weak sister, a stern old crow, and Miss Abigail. Miss Abby's appearance had nothin' to do with it. Why, the decision was unanimous by the members of the committee!"

"I think Pa's protesting too much. What do you think, Will?" Jeremiah asked, winking at Lizzie's father.

"Don't want to 'pear too hasty," Will said, pondering the matter, "but he could be doin' just that."

"Well! I never! Miss Abby's looks never entered into it a'tall. I sized her up as a good Christian woman who'd do her duty by our young'uns. Didn't make me no nevermind if she was pretty, plain, or somewheres in-between. And I'd have been as satisfied with a feller—iffen he'd measured up like Miss Abby did."

When everyone laughed at his vehement denials, Alton kept on with his futile explanation.

"I tell you, I didn't even notice that she was favor'ble to look at. Though now that you're bringin' it to Rory's attention, Lizzie, she did have awful purty yeller hair—" He thought some more. "Yep, she's a fine figger of a woman."

"So you did notice?" Jem teased.

"Maybe *now,* young feller, but not *then!*"

Fanny and Lizzie exchanged delighted smiles when it appeared that Alton Wheeler might be coming to life again. He was much too young, they had both said often, to spend the rest of his life without the love of a good woman.

As it was, Alton was suddenly awash in confusing and long forgotten emotions. But he was telling his friends the truth. Until that moment at Lizzie's table, he'd given little thought to Miss Abby's physical charms.

"Poor Miss Abigail doesn't have a chance with Rory, anyway," Alton heard Lizzie rattle on in a teasing lilt. Then her voice took on a dismal tone. "I'm afraid he's smitten by Judith Blye . . . or . . . is it Melinda Nash?"

"Lizzie! That's enough!" Rory yelped, glowering at his sister.

Lizzie giggled with glee and defiantly snapped her dishtowel in his direction to signify that she wasn't the least bit daunted by her little brother.

"Aha, so Melly it is!" she crowed triumphantly. "Well, at least she's a decent sort . . . which is more than I can say for her big sister, Carrie." She wrinkled her nose and gave a haughty sniff. "Whatever happened to the girl after she ran off with that travelin' salesman, anyway?" Lizzie didn't wait for an answer. "Take my advice, Rory, and don't do like Jeremiah and lose your gal by courtin' too slow like he did Carrie Nash."

Jem playfully tugged at Lizzie's apron string. "Now, Liz, aren't you glad I *did?*"

She laid a loving hand on his shoulder.

"I give thanks for that ever' day. I just wish *everybody* could be as happy as we are, darlin'. 'Specially those close to our heart 'n' hearth—"

She glanced at her father-in-law to see if he was listening, and didn't know whether to feel relieved or put out with him when her pointed words appeared lost on him. He was staring broodingly into his cup, his thoughts a million miles away.

Or was it only a mile and a half, Lizzie wondered, at the teacherage where Miss Abby lived?

"I think Pa Wheeler's attracted to Miss Abby," Lizzie told Jem when all of their dinner guests had gone home. "What Ma 'n' I are doin' seems to be workin'. Slow 'n' steady, I'll warrant, but that's better'n nothin'."

"Liz, I've seen that look in your eyes before. It's something you've got in common with Birdie and Mavis. You're about to get mulish about something. Don't barge in, sweetheart, where angels fear to tread. You know, sometimes when we try to help things along, we can do more harm than good."

"Ummm . . . maybe. But I only want Pa Wheeler to be happy again. He needs a good woman to love and to love him back. I think Miss Abby's the perfect match for your pa. So does Mama. And we're goin' to do everythin' in our power to see to it that it happens!"

"Well, don't leave the will of the Lord out of it," Jem reminded her.

"We're ahead of ya, Jem. Ma and I have been rememberin' Miss Abby and Pa Wheeler in our prayers real reg'lar. You've got to admit, we haven't seed your pa so quiet and thoughty since . . . since your mama died bearin' Molly and Marissa."

"Really?" Jeremiah inquired, his tone bland. "I hadn't noticed."

"Men! Sure as I'm standin' here," Lizzie mused, "somethin's goin' on in Alton Wheeler's mind . . . somethin' big, I'm thinkin'."

45

"Any ideas what it might be?" Jem asked, his eyes crinkling at the corners.

"At the moment, no. But you mark my words, Jeremiah Stone, I'm aimin' to find out!"

"Liz, honey, listen to me, will you? Just let Pa be, all right? Don't worry the situation like a terrier pup ragging a rat in the corncrib. Quit trying to work miracles on your own. If Alton and Miss Abby are meant to be, it'll work out. If not, it won't. It's as simple as that."

"But Jem—," Lizzie protested, biting back the thought that she was as tired of waiting for Alton to discover romance with Miss Abby as she was weary of waiting to conceive a new little life with Jem.

He put his arm around her. "Liz, I know your intentions are the purest and best. But did it ever occur to you that your scheming might actually be getting in the way of love? How would you like it if someone from the outside meddled in our lives? Do unto other folks, Lizzie, as you'd want them to do unto you. Be patient, Liz."

Lizzie made a face. "Oh . . . be patient this, be patient that! By Jove and by golly, Jeremiah Stone, I'm sick and tired of bein' patient, patient, *patient!*"

When she glared at him in sudden fury, he realized his gently chiding words had struck sparks, igniting her fury.

"My sweet, I don't think you've ever drawn a patient breath in your life, but let me see." Jeremiah pretended to wrack his brain, then he shook his head. "Nope! I can't remember one incidence of patience."

He expected her to laugh along with him, but he was startled when Lizzie's eyes brimmed with quick tears.

"*Wait!* I'm *tired* of waiting for things I want so bad, Jem. It's like my prayers go unheard. Is the Lord punishin' us . . . me . . . for marryin' so soon after Harmon died?"

Jem looked as if he'd been slapped, and he paled with the realization that Lizzie was dead serious and that his bantering words had only made things worse.

"Don't talk like that!" he whispered.

Lizzie gave Jem a wild-eyed look. "Well, why not? The truth's for tellin', just like Mama says. So is that what's happened? Is God punishin' me? Is that why no child has been conceived since I weaned Harmony onto a cup?"

"No!" Jeremiah thundered.

"Then why?" Lizzie's tone was plaintive. "I want a baby, Jem. Your baby. We've tried. I've prayed . . . but nothin'. Nothin' but disappointment."

"You pray, Liz," he said more softly, "and God hears. But you must remember, darlin', the Lord knows what is best for us, and that's what He wants to give us. Sometimes He says yes. Sometimes He says no, and because we haven't gotten what we want, we believe He hasn't heard—"

Lizzie's face crumpled. "We've both prayed for a baby, Jem, but a wee one's been denied us. I'm healthy. I've borne other children. Then why is the Lord sayin' no?"

"We can't presume to know God's mind, Liz. But you didn't let me finish. Sometimes the Lord is saying neither yes nor no. Sometimes, it's 'Wait.' "

Jem drew Lizzie to him, and she wilted in his arms.

" 'Wait' again! Oh, well," she sighed, "guess we can't be choosin' what happens. Guess we just have to take what comes."

"Oh, Liz—" Jem cuddled her close. "—you're so impetuous and impulsive and impatient. Maybe the Lord's just trying to help you learn how to bide your time."

"Well, at least, this time next year—" Lizzie straightened her shoulders, her chin jutting defiantly. "—Miss Abby and

Alton Wheeler will be married, or my name ain't Lizzie Stone!"

"See what I mean, Liz? You've got it all planned out, haven't you?" Jeremiah asked, bemused.

"Of course," Lizzie admitted in a light tone and gave Jem a hug as she dried her tears. "Can I help it if I want Alton and Miss Abby to be as happy as we are? You are happy with me, Jeremiah, ain't you?"

In answer, Jem gave a soft, almost exasperated groan.

"Happier than you'll ever know, sweetheart. You're everything I want. Everything I need in a woman."

Moved, she took his hand and brought it to her lips, pressed a kiss into his callused palm, and closed his fingers tightly around it.

"In fact, I love you so much," he whispered, "that I could probably even be talked into doing a bit of dabbling to help you womenfolk with your matchmaking. I expect your pa could be pressed into service, too, if you asked him."

Lizzie laughed with delight.

"You did see it, then, didn't you?"

Jeremiah nodded slowly. "I've seen the wanting on Miss Abby's face every now and again. And I saw Pa's eyes light up when he looked at her this noon."

"It's clear to all of us women that Miss Abby's sweet on Pa," Lizzie said. "And I think, with a little careful convincin', he could see that he's well on the way to bein' madly in love with her, too!"

"Lord willing," Jeremiah said, "I do believe you're right."

Lizzie's head was cradled against Jem's chest, and she listened to his heart thud beneath her ear as he murmured his own words of devotion. But a moment later, she was prying herself from his embrace. Her mouth worked, but no sounds came forth, and a patina of terror glazed her eyes.

"Sometimes I'm so happy it plumb scares me, Jem! That maybe that's why we ain't been blessed with more young'uns . . . 'cause there's tragedy just 'round the corner."

Jeremiah flinched, betraying his awareness of the same unpleasant premonition.

"Lizzie! Don't talk like that," he scolded in a hoarse whisper. "Don't even think like that! Think of happy things."

And taking his advice, she thought of happy things, purposely setting her tongue to outtalk the frightening thoughts that came when she was still.

"I've 'bout got the boys' new shirts sewed for them to wear to Miss Abby's Christmas pageant."

"They'll be handsome lads."

"And I made little Katie a new dress just like one for Harmony. Mama's doin' some o' her fancywork for 'em, tattin' collars. It's dreadful expensive for Alton to get clothes in town from the seamstress. And we wanted Katie to have a new dress like most of the other young'uns."

"It's difficult for Pa. It'd be hard for any man. We—we just don't see."

"Miss Abby sees," Lizzie stated confidently. "And her hands just itch to tend to the Wheeler girls like a lovin' mama." She gave an optimistic smile. "Alton and Miss Abby will be together in the same room the night of the Christmas pageant . . . 'n' I'm goin' to have 'em both here Christmas Eve. Then Mama plans to invite 'em for Christmas Day . . . 'n' after that, there's Valentine's Day—"

"You're a plotter and a schemer," Jem sighed, throwing up his hands in mock surrender.

But Lizzie wasn't hearing anything he said, so busily was her fertile mind spinning the web that would draw the lovers together.

"On Valentine's Day, we'll see that we get Miss Abby and

your pa together. I could bake and frost some sugar cookies with red icin' . . . and cut 'em out in the shape of hearts. By golly, Jeremiah Stone, that's exactly what I'll do!" Lizzie cheerfully planned. "In fact, I'll bake enough for the whole school. You and Pa can make yourselves scarce—maybe go to Effingham on business—and I can have Pa Wheeler bring the twins by to help me make cookies. He won't turn me down since he wants the girls to have a woman's touch . . . then I'll offer to keep the babies if he'll deliver the cookies to the teacherage since neither you nor Pa can do the honors—"

"I give up! I give up! We'll do it, Liz!"

"Lord willin', it'll work out just as I'm hopin' and prayin'," she said, and gave a dreamy sigh.

It did work out exactly as Lizzie had planned.

Alton and Miss Abby soon found themselves regularly paired in the company of Salt Creek's residents. It was clear to everyone that Miss Abby was smitten with Alton and, though he would have denied it, that he found her company very pleasant. Still, from his actions, people suspected that he believed himself too old, too unsophisticated, too uneducated for the likes of the pretty schoolmarm, and he steadfastly refused to take any action that would suggest he was courting her.

Even little Katie Wheeler, who loved her teacher and had decided that she wanted her for her very own mama, had done what she could to bring the matter to her pa's attention.

He had at first scolded Katie for interfering. Then, since the child had created a situation that demanded an explanation, Alton had found himself in the schoolroom alone with Miss Abby. And by the end of the afternoon, the two had returned to the Stone farmplace to announce their intentions to wed when the school term ended.

"God has heard our prayers for Miss Abby and Pa

Wheeler!" Lizzie rejoiced as she and Fanny laughingly embraced after seeing the couple off to the teacherage. "Now, if He would only hear my prayers for—"

"What's that, daughter?" Fanny asked. "What's that you're sayin'?"

"Nothin', Mama," Lizzie sighed. "Jem's right. I need to learn patience, not want everythin' at once. Havin' Alton and Miss Abby announcin' their intentions gives me joy enough to last 'til Jem and I have our own blessed news to tell—"

chapter
4

"MY! WASN'T IT a nice weddin'?" Lizzie sighed as she and her mother gathered Lizzie's brood and prepared to depart for home after the celebration of Alton and Miss Abigail's marriage vows. "If only they'd had a photographer take a picture of 'em so's they'd always know what they looked like on this day."

"Oh, Lizzie-girl, you and your hankerin' for picture-takin'."

"Now, Mama, don't try to tell me that you ain't as proud as punch of that fam'ly picture. It was worth everythin' it cost me."

Fanny laughed as she recalled that day in the hog wallow after which she had shampooed her daughter's long hair four times to rid it of the nose-wrinkling scent.

"I should hope to say it was!" Fanny agreed, chuckling, as she laid a wrinkled hand against her daughter's smooth cheek. "That fair was a happy time for us all . . . 'n' witnessin' Alton and Miss Abby pledgin' their vows has given this community another good mem'ry. Don't they make a fine-lookin' couple, though, with him so tall, dark, 'n' handsome and her so tiny and blonde?"

"Miss Abby was the purtiest bride I've ever seed!" Lizzie said, then frowned. "*Miss* Abby? What're we goin' to call her now that she's wed to Pa Wheeler? Miz Wheeler sounds so stiff and unfriendly-like. But with her bein' the young'uns' teacher, callin' her by her first name don't sound respectful."

"I don't know, lambie. For the life o' me, she may always be Miss Abby to me—'n' ever'one—'specially since she's agreed to continue on as the schoolmarm for next year, that is, 'less God has other plans for her—"

"As I see it, the committee had best start in lookin' for a replacement," Lizzie ventured. "The way Miss Abby loves young'uns—and with Molly and Marissa big girls now—she may have a powerful hankerin' for a wee babe of her very own."

Lizzie's own longings were written on her face.

Fanny turned away, biting her lip to keep from speaking out. Perhaps, one day soon she would find a way to break the news gently to Lizzie that, in the wake of Jeremiah's illness, there would be no more children. Furthermore, she prayed that her beloved daughter's faith was now rooted deeply enough to hold her fast through the storm of that bitter disappointment.

May flitted by, gay and colorful as the butterflies that dotted the sky. The streams ran swift with runoff from warm rains that encouraged grass to shoot up thick and lush, and caused wildflowers in the timber to bloom in profusion.

June arrived fresh and hopeful as the dazzling white blackberry blossoms that promised a full harvest if the rains came.

The Fourth of July dawned hot and sultry, with the air sticking to the skin like damp wool. But the weather didn't keep the members of the Salt Creek community from their annual patriotic festivities.

Talk was of the relentless hot spell that had begun early in June, instead of following the anticipated summer rains.

At play, the children panted for breath as they ran, too overheated to squeal. Even so, they romped on while mothers scolded, reminding them to stop and rest, lest they collapse from the heat. A few of the less hardy ones already lay prostrate on the prickly grass, shivering despite the temperature, their eyes glassy, faces flushed.

The women fared little better. Sweat trickled to the creases of their necks and ran down to collect in the boning of their corsets. Discreetly withdrawing linen handkerchiefs from their basques, they dabbed daintily at the rivulets of perspiration, and tucked the damp cloths back into place. Only seconds later found them modestly retrieving hankies again to remove yet another film of moisture.

In the shade of the great oaks and sycamores, the men lounged lazily, chatting and whittling. A game of horseshoes was underway. Robust cheers went up when a ringer clanged noisily against the iron spike, and a chorus of groans when a shot went far afield. Though the menfolk seemed to be taking the mounting temperatures in stride, their straw hats were soon pressed into service as fans to hurry along the hot summer breeze.

As the morning wore on, some of the mothers found themselves growing short-tempered, piqued by small children who tangled underfoot, scrapping and whining, or by older youngsters who persisted in playing too hard. From years of sad experience, the mothers knew that just as warmth causes all living things to grow, heat can kill.

Finally, seeing the ladies' struggle, some of the men left their game and improvised an awning to shelter them from the wilting sun. Others did what they could to corral obstreperous children while their mamas laid out the picnic lunch. But, to the consternation of the cooks, prize frostings melted, running down the sides of the cakes to puddle in the pan, and they despaired of ever getting the meal on the plank tables before the food was completely ruined.

When the dinner gong sounded at last, they prayed first for rain and respite from the heat, even before blessing the bountiful feast. The food, along with gallons of lemonade, kept cool in a nearby spring, revived the picknickers' spirits. But the combined effects of the ample meal and the breathless temperatures soon took their toll. Many of the youngsters napped in the shade while their parents whiled away the long afternoon in idle conversation.

Late in the day, Lizzie smoothed out a blanket and with Harmony in her arms, settled onto it, grateful that the sun sinking in the west was bringing a blessed drop in the temperature.

As the sky grew dusky, however, mosquitoes came spiraling out from the undersides of leaves, and soon children were fussing, their mamas swatting at the pesky insects. Again, the men came to the rescue, lighting wheat straw smudges. The pleasantly tangy smoke wafted over the area, holding the mosquitoes at bay so that the revelers could continue their celebration until bedtime.

"Takin' a moment of rest by yourself, darlin'?" Fanny asked.

"Uh-huh! Join me, Mama, while Harmony's nappin'?" Lizzie asked, and patted the quilt beside her.

"Don't mind iffen I do."

Lizzie stretched out a strong hand to help her mother, and the older woman settled herself onto the coverlet like a fussy hen, squatting exactingly into a nest.

"Ain't that purty?" Lizzie sighed, listening as some of the women harmonized while the men played their fiddles and Alton drew out his harmonica. At his side, Miss Abby

56

produced her own instrument and played, too. Content, Lizzie hummed along softly so as not to arouse Harmony, who had curled up with her head pillowed in her mama's lap.

When the area band paused to consult over the next selection, the night was eerily still.

"Listen to the rustlin' of the cornstalks," Fanny said, swatting at a mosquito that had slipped through the line of defense.

Lizzie cocked her head.

The corn in the plot across the trail crackled dryly beneath the gentle wind blowing through central Illinois. The breeze was hot and constant those days, parching everything in its path. Pale, dusty leaves curled upward as if pleading with the heavens for rain. But during the hot days they wilted, with no hope of a reprieve from the searing sun.

Already it had been necessary to ration water from the cistern. Lizzie, along with the other women, was mindful to use even dirty washwater to give relief to trees and plants and to ration drinking and bath water until the Lord saw fit to send them the rain they so desperately needed.

The evening wore on, centered, as usual, on the stultifying heat and the frightening lack of rain. At length, one of the men raised the prospect of hiring a rain man to perform his strange rites and incantations in the hope of breaking the drought.

His suggestion produced some concerned frowns, while other worried farmers urged the fellow to speak up. In all fairness, they said, they should hear what he had to say.

Normally a shy man, and alone in the world as he tilled his plot of land without a helpmate or children, he was flustered at being thrust front and center, with the attention of everyone in the community riveted on him.

"Don't know much about it," he admitted, "but I've heard

tell it can work. If you get a good rain man—one who knows what he's doin'—he can get the storm clouds to appear and needed moisture to fall. It costs dear, though, I'm sure. Anyone able to arrange such a miracle could charge handily and would earn every penny—"

When he ended his speech, there was not a sound. No one ventured a question. No one offered a comment. Rather than suffer the embarrassing silence, the man hurried on.

"I reckon if we were to try, we could find somebody—in Effingham, anyway—who'd know of a rain man in St. Louis, Chicago, or even Indianapolis. If we'd each kick in a bit o' jack, we could finance it." The young farmer's tone was plaintive, but hope-filled. "Wh—what d'ya think?"

The sound of feet shuffling on the dry, stubby grass drowned out the agonized rustling of the corn. Then the menfolk looked at each other, searching the faces of friends and neighbors, reading their answers in a stance, the unyielding set of a jaw.

"I know you mean well, friend," Jeremiah spoke up, "but we don't believe in bypassing the will of the Lord, looking for miracles that don't come through the power of His name. Anything else is deception."

"We have no need of lyin' miracles," Will put in. "I agree with Jeremiah."

"Scripture warns of a sorry plight for those who consult diviners, necromancers, soothsayers, 'n' the like," Alton reminded them all. "And I'd say a rain man, no matter how nice and friendly the feller is, falls smack-dab in the middle of that list somewheres."

"An' that's the gospel truth!" Fanny piped up from the cluster of women who had gathered to listen but remained silent as their menfolk wrestled with the decision.

Will Preston hitched his suspenders and stepped forward, placing a gentle hand on the young stranger's shoulder.

"We 'preciate your concern for our predic'ment, young feller," he said. "And we *will* get rain! We'll find a reg'lar gullywasher bestowed on us . . . when the good Lord's ready to send it our way. Until then, we can only wait 'n' have faith. An' we can pray. But we won't *pay!*"

"No, there'll be no collections to hire a rain man," said Lemont Gartner, "although 'twere it that simple, I'd ride to Effingham myself, have a bank draft writ out, and buy a thunderstorm for the lot o' us! But there's more to it than that . . . more at stake, too."

"I—I'm sorry. I meant no offense," the young man apologized.

"'Course you didn't," Fanny said. "In times like these, desperate people do desperate things, son. We've all had our temptations to take shortcuts to get what we want, rather than be patient and wait for God's timin'. 'Stead of turnin' to our bank accounts or fruit jars full o' money chucked up in the cupboard, we need to turn to the Good Book."

There was a murmuring ripple of discussion, but the suggestion was dismissed as unworthy for a God-fearing people, and eventually they turned to other topics of conversation. But it was only with effort that the lively tone of the day was recaptured.

Looking about her, Lizzie was suddenly overwhelmed by the memory of the barn raising held for her and Harmon Childers on this very date. Yet it seemed, oddly enough, as if all that had taken place centuries before.

Lizzie suddenly felt old beyond her years.

Day by day, she decided as she mulled over her circumstances, life was generally tolerable. *Spread out over an extended period of time, one is able to bear things that would be impossible to*

59

accept without rebelling if they'd arrived all at once. But lumped together and not parceled out over the long haul, life could too easily become more than a mere mortal could endure, she thought. She'd certainly borne her share of trials and tribulation woven in among the days of triumph.

Even though the night was hot and the air was suffocating in its closeness, Lizzie shivered, and goosebumps rippled across her exposed flesh when she remembered Pa Wheeler's warning words condemning soothsayers and the like.

She squirmed as if some evil thing had slithered over her in the darkness, then crawled away to search out some other victim of its beguiling messages.

Once, when she'd been in Effingham, she'd been fiercely tempted to seek out a gypsy fortuneteller who lived in a squalid shanty on the poor side of town and who plied her ungodly trade in exchange for a few coins.

Lizzie had saved up some money from the farm crops, for she was a thrifty sort, and Jeremiah denied her nothing within reason. Not that she'd ever asked for anything that wasn't practical. Still, she felt that if she wanted to spend a dab of money to purchase peace of mind, he wouldn't object.

She'd planned to slip away to town, hand over her coin, and ask but one question of the tarot card-dealing, tea-leaf-reading, crystal-ball-gazing woman. One answer about the future would satisfy her.

But now she was glad she had not given in to temptation and sought from dark powers what would yet be revealed through the light of the Lord and His Word. She would wait patiently and prayerfully for the answer to her most fervent prayer. *Besides,* she thought, *sometimes it's best not to know!*

Knowing what was in store, how could a body bear the anticipation of some dread disaster, drawing nearer day by day, hour by hour, moment by moment? Why, consumed with the specter of sorrow, it would be impossible to enjoy life at all! To live thus would be to despair. A life without hope.

"It's so much better to live with hope for the morrow," Lizzie whispered to herself.

"Thinkin' of the past, honey?" Fanny asked quietly.

"K—kind of hard not to, Ma. Been thinkin' 'bout life. Day by day, it sort of swirls by—like water in Salt Creek rollin' on to spill into the Little Wabash not far away. And then those many drops of water are carried to the Big Wabash—so far away I've never been there. An' it goes on and on 'til it ends up in the Ohio River, then the mighty Mississip', and maybe even the Gulf of Mexico, mergin' with the ocean. Why, that same little drop of water may someday wash up on some distant shore in a foreign place."

"My! You're right serious-headed tonight, gal," Fanny declared. "What's come over you?"

Lizzie shrugged. "Can't help thinkin' how people come 'n' go in our lives. Friends pass away, new ones come along to make our acquaintance . . . sorta like threads weavin' in 'n' out in a colorful tapestry. But it's a tapestry without beginnin' or end . . . leastways, not so's we can see it. All of this weavin' in and weavin' out . . . some folks die . . . young'uns are born—" Lizzie faced her mother. "Life . . . it's just always changin', ain't it?"

Fanny, too, grew thoughtful. For a while, the two women sat in companionable silence, listening to the old-time melodies that blossomed in the air.

"I reckon you're right, child," she said at last. "We're all a-changin' . . . from the minute we're born to the last breath we draw . . . changin' and growin'. But it won't be 'til we're with the Lord, I 'spect, that we can hope to understand what was kind of fuzzy and confusin' to us while we was livin' here on this earth—"

Once again the two women embraced the silence until Lizzie broke it again.

"I was so proud of Jeremiah this evenin'," she whispered as Harmony shifted, sighed heavily, then snuggled down in her sleep. "When there was talk of a rain man, and he stood up and spoke his piece, I could've busted with joy, knowin' that I was wed to such a righteous man."

Fanny gave a soft chuckle. "Ah . . . no prouder'n I was of your dear papa, Lizzie . . . 'n' I 'spect Miss Abby was o' Alton."

Lizzie nodded. "But change, like we was discussin' a whipstitch ago, Mama, it's so gradual you scarce see it comin'. I—it's kind of scary, Ma."

"What're you gettin' at?" Fanny asked, peering through the growing darkness. "You can't fool your old ma. Somethin's troublin' you, daughter. What is it?"

Lizzie shook her head, unable to speak. She swallowed hard and tried again.

"It's about . . . Pa—"

That was all she could manage before her voice and emotions failed her and she bit down on her lip . . . hard.

"What about your pa?"

Silence spiraled once more before Lizzie could force any speech past the dry lump lodged solidly in her throat.

"He's *old,*" she cried in a soft whisper. "I've always thought of Pa as young . . . ageless . . . like he was when I was little. Now he's . . . *old 'n' failin'.*"

Fanny reached across and took Lizzie's strong young hand in her gnarled grip and gave it a squeeze.

"But you're a child no longer, Lizzie. Life has been passin' by for Pa 'n' me, too, as it has for you," she reminded her.

"Just like the seasons of the year, lambie, we go through phases of livin'. You passed through the springtime of your life when you were a carefree child. Now you're movin' full into your summer years, Lizzie. But you'll be surprised how soon autumn comes like it did for Pa and me—"

Fanny sighed and shifted her weight to rest her aching bones more easily on the quilt, then gave her daughter a sidelong glance, choosing her next words carefully. "Now it's wintertime for us, child, and I don't mind tellin' you, it's an uphill path. We're bone weary, tired o' livin'. If 'tweren't for the promises o' God urgin' us on, remindin' us we're still here to do His biddin', then I 'spect we'd as leave lie down and die . . . and find our eternal rest."

"Mama! Don't talk like that!" Lizzie moaned. With sudden clarity she saw the day when her mother, so full of wise counsel, so warm and solid beside her, would no longer be with her. "This is s'posed to be a happy day!"

"Lizzie . . . Lizzie—," Fanny soothed, "don't take on so, girl. Facin' the truth can free you up to live content, knowin' you've no regrets over things done . . . or left undone."

Lizzie stared straight ahead as the jumbled insights were sorted and stored away in her mind. Only the brusque, jerky motion of her arm bore witness to the fact that she was swiping away scalding tears.

"You're talkin' about Pa, ain't you?" she whispered.

"In a roundabout way, I reckon I am, Lizzie, though the same truth applies to all us mortals. We're born to die, y'know, to face our Maker and account to Him for how we've used our lives. So I try to live each day as if 'tis my last!"

Tenderly Lizzie put her arm around her mother, feeling a sense of intimate closeness she hadn't enjoyed to such fullness in years.

"Your memory will *never* die, Mama," Lizzie promised.

"Why, when Jem 'n' I start havin' our own young'uns, there'll be a son by the name of Will—just as I've told you before—and a girl, maybe even one with hair the color of gingersnaps like yours, named Fanchon . . . after you—"

"Oh, Lizzie—" Fanny's voice was devoid of the joy Lizzie had expected the happy announcement to bring. "Face it, darlin'! Accept this disappointin' fact same as you're gettin' used to the idea that you won't always have your pa 'n' me close by."

Lizzie whipped around. "What are you talkin' about, Ma?"

Fanny gave a wry laugh. "You haven't heard a word o' what I've tried to tell you all these many months, have you, child?"

"Well, I've—"

"*Mumps!* They do things to a man sometimes, Lizzie, when they migrate from the jaws as they did with your Jem. You'll carry no child of Jeremiah's, mark my words."

The news struck Lizzie a stunning blow.

"Oh, Mama, no!" she cried with sudden blinding insight.

"Be brave, Lizzie, and trustin'. For it's the will of God, and He don't make mistakes."

"But Jem's wanted a baby so bad . . . maybe even more'n me!" she protested. "How's he goin' to—"

Fanny patted Lizzie, subduing her to silence. "Maybe, lambie, that's 'cause your wish is his command, 'n' he knows a babe has been your fondest dream. The man loves your young'uns as his own. He don't need children from his own loins to know the joys of bein' a father."

In the moment that Lizzie realized that there would be no child for her and Jem, she chose to trust in the Lord and shook free of the desire that had scarcely left her mind or heart for all the days of their marriage.

"Well . . . someday," Lizzie said, swallowing, her voice growing stronger, brave, "there'll be *grandbabies!*"

Fanny laughed heartily and gave Lizzie a quick hug. "Lots and lots of 'em. An' it's one o' my sweetest hopes that I'll live long enough to dandle 'em all on my knee!"

chapter
5

THE INDEPENDENCE DAY celebration ended with the members of the Salt Creek community standing quietly, hands folded, heads bowed, as Will Preston lifted his voice to pray humbly once again for the rain that they so badly needed. He also sought respite from the terrible heat that was robbing their bodies of vitality, bringing hardship to the livestock, crushing their spirits, and even causing them to forget momentarily the Lord's providence as they suffered their human woes.

"Amen . . . ," the crowd softly murmured as they turned away, wending to their individual horse- or mule-drawn conveyances.

But in coming days there was no end in sight.

As July rolled on, grinding them asunder, threatening to soon become the dog days of August, the dreaded heat continued. Livestock dropped dead, and while no one in the community had passed on because of the relentless heat, there were those, including Will, who suffered sickly spells that folks believed were aggravated by the soaring temperatures.

Sprinklings of rain—no more than would fill a teacup per acre, men grumbled—only dampened hope for the drenching shower that was needed to replenish the earth, refill cisterns and rain barrels, and make Salt and Bishop Creeks swell to

67

more than a trickle, as clay creek banks cracked and curled beneath the kiln-like summer sun.

People, despite their best efforts, suffered, but livestock was in dire need.

Sows with their broods of suckling pigs at their sides lay in dried wallows, the earth as hard-baked as pottery. The sows panted for breath, and their piglets wheezed and weakly mewled, all of them too exhausted from the heat to flick an ear or a tail to discourage tenacious flies that seemed to proliferate.

When farmers poured precious water into their troughs, the heat-weary pigs found the strength to gallop forth, but then they fought over the water until they often ended up splashing or spilling more than they drank. And the parched earth swallowed the moisture before they could lap it from the ground.

Farmers lashed barrels to buckboards and wagons, drove to the creek, and with shovels and tumble-bugs worked to widen what pools existed so that more water would collect in the wide, deep areas between riffling shallows.

Daily, folks dipped water from Salt Creek and carried it in wooden-staved barrels to their upland farms and ladled out the precious moisture to quench the livestock's thirst with brackish water unfit for humans to drink.

Cows grazed on the parched pastures, but the grass remained stubbly and tough, containing few nutrients because there was no rain to encourage growth to restore what they had consumed. Soon the cows' ribs showed through their dull hides. Rumps became bony protrusions from which hung limp tails. Their udders shrank, wrinkling, as the trauma of the unceasing temperatures caused them to go dry, and the calves at their sides bawled with hunger and butted their heads against the cows' bags to try to produce spurts of milk.

The horses plodded listlessly through their work. The equine beasts dropped weight so quickly that their owners looked at them with alarm and helplessly wrung their hands.

What if the horses died—however would they cope? How would they work? A man could scarcely yoke himself and beg his woman to tend the plow as he leaned into the harness and hove ahead to try to till the stubborn earth!

Animals began to perish in the heat. Word spread that thousands upon thousands of horses in the midwestern states had dropped dead from the heat, as had cows, pigs, and sheep who suffered beneath the weight of wool. With their very livelihood at stake, the men had no choice but to harness up their horses and work them as they dared, praying for the best.

The summer jobs were mowing and raking what pitifully little fodder remained to be harvested beneath the blistering sun. Then there was always cultivating corn to be done and pulling of the grain binders. . . .

Many farmers ended up cutting the grain by moonlight. They pressed their enthusiastic children into scampering ahead with lanterns containing precious coal oil to light the way so that they could labor in the darkness in an attempt to spare their horses and themselves the worst ravages of the noonday sun.

There was little sleep at night and almost none by day when the sun was blinding, as bright as a silver dollar hanging in the sky, radiating a heat that seemed almost white in its hotness.

Some days a team could only cultivate an acre of corn. But in a tree-lined patch, with no breeze stirring, it was too hot to exist in the burning sun for the length of time it required to do more than that. Men and their beasts of burden returned to their cabins, driven from the fields, the men gushing sweat, as the horses coughed, panted, then shivered as precious buckets of water were ladled over dusty coats in hope that a beast's internal temperature could be reduced to safe levels.

Alton spent almost every waking moment tending to Doc and Dan while Jem fussed over his mules, more desperate in his attempts, after the family horse, Daisy, an aging mare that had belonged to Harmon, was found dead, stiff-legged, bloated in the heat when the family arose one morning.

Sweat and tears had mingled on Jem's face as he hitched Birdie and Mavis to the dead horse, dragged the carcass out into a clearing, ricked firewood upon it, then collected dried leaves, grass, and twigs to kindle an inferno, and stood sentry to prevent the hapless spread of embers to the nearby parched earth where it could create a fire that would endanger the area.

Meanwhile, the sleek, dark buzzards, fattened on the dregs of death, circled in the sky, their shapes casting giant black shadows over the hostile earth. The carrion birds cawed loudly, swooped low, but then the intense heat drove them away from the offal, as the stomach-wrenching scent of burning flesh plumed into the sky.

Jem was shaking with weakness, his strength drained from exertion in the heat, but he knew that he dared not leave the horse to rot beneath the sun, a haven for flies and vultures. The threat of cholera was too great, a further plague they dared not invite. . . .

Through it all, Lizzie bore her lot without complaint.

Even when she had reason to weep—she managed to smile. She kept her spirits up, praying to the Lord for strength to do so when she actually wished only to fall down on the feather tick and cry until there were no more tears.

Lizzie had concluded that in such trying, tense times, her family would receive their attitudes for the day from her. She was aware the onus was on her. She would set the mood for all of them, from Jeremiah on down to Harmony, through her actions and attitudes, be they happy or sad, cheerful or curt, protesting, or optimistically accepting.

So Lizzie chose to be joyous.

Even in the face of adversity, she gave heartfelt thanks. She pointed out their great fortune that she had a bounty of canned goods left from earlier years to see them through until the following year's growing season, and pray God, that it would not be as barren as the current one.

Through it all, Lizzie knew a serene happiness.

Fanny noticed a change in her girl. The young woman's impulsiveness seemed tempered by thoughtful, far-sighted restraint. Her zeal was subdued by honestly recognizing the possible consequences wrought by too hasty action, or an ill-chosen remark that could leave her repenting at leisure if she were foolhardy enough to act on her sometimes rash ideas.

"There's a change in you, Liz," Jeremiah remarked one late summer evening after the terrible heat had passed and seasonal climes and appreciated rain had returned to the area.

"Really?"

"It's happened so slow, I'm not even sure when it occurred," Jem mused. "All I know is that you're a different woman from the gal that I married. I can't quite put my finger on just exactly how it is, or why it is." He hugged Lizzie hard, then kissed the tip of her nose. "But know that I like it a lot. Immensely so. Not that it diminishes how much I loved you when we married. But I somehow love you even more now. So much more."

Lizzie smiled and patted Jem's cheek. "When we stop a-changin', Jeremiah, I reckon we'll be dead, hmmmm? And then we'll be changin' too, from our earthly ways as we get used to partakin' of heavenly matters. I expect mayhap we'll *never* stop changin' 'n' learning and enjoyin' the ways of greater wisdom. . . ."

Jeremiah thought it over and gave a content laugh. "For an uneducated woman, Liz, you're awful smart sometimes." He drew Lizzie back into his arms and nuzzled the hollow of her throat as she lifted her arms behind his head to clasp her hands at the nape of his neck and hold him close.

"Smart enough to marry you," she reminded.

Jem's gaze grew misty with adoration. "I love you so much, Elizabeth Stone, that . . . that . . . that sometimes it plumb scares me."

Lizzie stiffened in his arms.

She inched away from him. Her eyes searched his face.

"Scares you?" she whispered, after swallowing hard, but even so she feared she was not quite able to hide the tremor that came into her tone. She hoped that she could shield from him the reason for the timbre so that he would not realize that she'd found sudden terror in knowing that her unspoken emotion matched his unexpected utterance.

"You mean . . . you feel like you're so happy that you're afraid something's going to try to ruin it? Ruin us? So we won't know such happiness? So we'll be tested? As tribulation will try to wrest us away from—" She couldn't finish the fearsome thought with her lips, but it screamed in her mind. *". . . wrest us from livin' our faith and offerin' witness to our children and the world!"*

Jeremiah looked surprised when Lizzie gave words to his deepest feelings and concerns, matters he'd not discussed even with another man.

"Well . . . yeah," he quietly admitted. "I've read the Book of Job, darlin', and I wonder how he could've withstood what he did. I consider what could happen to us, and I tremble at what we might face in the testin' of our faith."

"Oh, Jem . . . ," Lizzie murmured helplessly.

She bit her lip and then gave an anguished laugh to keep from bursting into tears. She dared not share with him the frightening admission that it had been like that for her, too!

Could they both be wrong?

Lizzie forced herself to present for him a happy-go-lucky grin. And a bantering joke was as quickly on her lips.

She was flooded with relief when she saw the dark wave of doubt ebb from Jem's face, and she knew that once again she'd succeeded at sparking his levity as her own had begun to flicker, threatening to become extinguished beneath a pall of fear.

Jeremiah responded by hugging her ferociously.

"You're always so happy, Liz. How do you do it? How do you manage? Your days are long, even longer'n mine, I have only the fields and livestock to worry about. You must concern yourself with everything. You'd have a right to rail and get snappish. But you stay as happy as a meadowlark. Seems to me it's like a miracle."

Lizzie's eyes danced. "Mayhap that it *is* a miracle. But I've figured out that the secret to happiness, Jem, is so simple. It's so very, very simple, that some folks pro'bly turn away from it, not realizing that something so priceless can be had for such little understandin' that even a child could fathom the concept."

She paused as she searched his face to ascertain the depth of his attention.

"See, now, the old Lizzie, the gal you married, well, she wanted things. That Lizzie constantly sought to lay plans, attempted to make things happen, wanted to work little ol' worldly miracles, and labored to make events happen so that those coveted dreams could come true. And sometimes they did—like with Alton 'n' Miss Abby gettin' hitched. But they'd probably have fallen in love and married iffen I hadn't so much as turned a tap to try 'n' arrange it."

Jeremiah laughed as she ran on with her unabashed self-assessment.

"Yes, you certainly did try to rule your private little world," he agreed. "But thank God you were a kind monarch, darlin', with your adoring subjects' best interests at heart."

Then he frowned, as if he were trying to recollect an exact date when that apt description of his beloved wife had ceased to be accurate and true.

"Now the new, the happy Lizzie, well, she doesn't do those things any more because this Liz knows that the secret of being happy is to merely *be content*."

"Be content?" he echoed, and his tone sounded vaguely disappointed as if that were too simple to be a viable philosophy of life.

"Yup! Bein' content means making yourself be perfectly satisfied with exactly what you have. So you're not hankerin' for more, nor wantin' less than the good Lord has seen fit to bestow on you moment by moment, day by day, year in, year out."

Jeremiah was silent then he gave Lizzie an adoring kiss. In his eyes was more love than Lizzie had ever seen before.

"It's a secret to be shared," Jeremiah murmured. "And I'm thankful you chose to present such knowledge to me. 'Be content—be happy.'"

"That's all there is to it," Lizzie whispered. "And I am, Jeremiah. I am so happy."

"We are," Jeremiah corrected.

"Yes," Lizzie sighed, content. Her lips touched Jem's. "For now and forever."

His lips claimed hers. She stroked the hair at the back of his neck as his arms tightened around her shoulders.

The spell—the precious moment—was shattered when Lester burst into the cabin. The door cracked against the inner wall, then was flung shut with such force that it shook the cabin upon its closure.

"Mama! Come quick! Uncle Rory's riding toward us—crying something awful—and whipping Grandpa's horse! Hurry, Ma—it must be something horrible's happened!"

Lizzie's heart stopped beating before it sped to a galloping pace.

She clutched at her skirts, skittered through the cabin door, and her feet flew over the stones lining the walk. Jem was a step behind. They saw Rory, wildly sobbing, whipping the horse, as the sorrel mare's hooves thundered over the clay ruts.

Lizzie wilted and fell into Jem's arms when the impact of the coming message hit her. "Oh, no! Jem—Papa's dead!"

Rory stumbled from the saddle, fell to the ground, and as the horse heaved and panted, Rory sobbed out the crushing truth. Will Preston had dropped dead of a stroke.

Lizzie knelt beside Rory. She hugged her distraught brother to her as he cried. He was steeped in grief but awash in fury.

"It can't be changed, Rory," she wept. "Papa's dead. Don't take on so!"

But Rory was inconsolable. He said things that Lizzie covered her ears so she would not hear. She turned away, a victim of her own heartbreak.

"Jeremiah, please tend to Rory if you would," she wept. "I must tell the children. We need to go to Mama. . . ."

"C'mon, Rory," Jem said, and gently eased him from the ground, helping him to catch his balance as the shorter man stabbed the earth with his peg leg. Then he collapsed against Jem.

Lizzie turned back, her face ashen, her eyes large with pleading. "Rory, please! We've a need to be strong for Mama's sake—and in respect for Pa's memory! The Lord gives 'n' the Lord takes away. You know that."

But Rory seemed without the will to reconcile himself to the reality of his pa's death.

Lizzie gathered the children around her and told of Will's passing. She wiped her eyes, squared her shoulders, then faced the tasks of packing necessary things to go be with her mother to help with the routines for a burying.

"Lester, be a man and tend to your brothers and little sister while your pa and I go to Mama. Rory, you and Jem can go up in the barn loft when we get to Mama's, and fetch down the burial box that Papa built."

They hurriedly proceeded to Fanny's farm where Miss Abby and Alton, who'd chanced to pass by, were present with the Widow Preston. With Lizzie's arrival, Alton excused himself to take the three Wheeler girls home while Miss Abby remained behind to help with laying out the dead.

Time passed in a blur of tears. Neighbors came to sit up with the dead and help bear the burden of grief with Will's family.

The grave was dug. The burial service was conducted.

One by one somber friends filed by, spaded up earth, and dropped it into the gaping chasm, paying their final respects.

Jem and Rory remained behind to close the grave.

Jem worked alone as Rory disappeared into the woods, a wounded thing in his hopeless, wracking, angry grief. Lizzie, so much like her mother, was stoic in her mourning.

Three days after Rory had arrived with the tragic news, Lizzie returned to her home after quiet moments with her mother, but Jem was not to be found.

Needing his companionship, Lizzie searched for him. He

was not in the field, nor was he with his precious mules, the valuable breeding stock now in residence in the pasture, with the coming year holding the promise of their first crop of mules.

Lizzie felt fear encircle her heart as the farm seemed eerily devoid of Jem's presence.

She was about to call for him—afraid her cry would be a hysterical shriek—when she heard thuds echoing from the shed.

Pound . . . pound . . . pound . . . pound!

The hollow sound was followed by the rasp of a handsaw chewing through hardwood planking.

"Jem?" she questioned as she stepped into the dimness of the shed. He looked up at her, his smile bidding her to enter.

She hesitated in the open door, poignant memories swirling around her, begging remembrance and identification. Then the truth assaulted her, and a huge lump welled in her throat as more tears stung her eyes, and she recalled the many scents that she so strongly associated with her beloved pa's carpentry efforts. . . .

The musty shed.

The tang of sawdust.

Sunlight slanting across the floor.

Falling from the plane's razor edge were golden curls of wood as tight as the sausage curls Mama had once upon a time created in Lizzie's unruly hair by binding her locks in rags.

Jem swallowed hard, then blinked fast and turned back to his work, carefully, painstakingly, measuring the length, again and again, the better to keep his wet eyes lowered from Lizzie's.

"Your pa gave me his fiddle," Jeremiah explained in a low whisper. "But I've seen fit to take upon myself his responsibility of always havin' a burial box on hand in case there's a need in the community."

"Oh Jem . . ."

Helplessly Lizzie began to weep, not with sorrow but with unbounded joy in the precious knowledge of Jem's reliability. He drew her to him, pulled a handkerchief from his hind pocket, mopped his brow, then swiped it to collect the moisture that had gathered in his eyes.

"Pa knew what he was doin' in giving you his fiddle, the source of his play 'n' pleasure, 'cause he knew you'd willingly accept the yoke of responsibility."

Lizzie burrowed into Jem's comforting embrace, weeping out the grief that had remained pent-up as she'd sought to be even more serene in her sorrow to make up for Rory's lack and hurtful rebellions.

"Someday, Liz," Jem said. "I'll be passin' on the fiddle to Lester. I'll teach him to play it—'n' the day will surely come when he'll hand it on down to his young'un, and instruct him in its mastering." He cleared his throat. "I think Will would like that. Expect that . . ."

"I know he would," Lizzie said. "He put the world that he left behind in good hands, Jem. The Lord's—'n' yours."

"We're all the richer for knowin' your pa, Liz."

"I can't be so grieving over Pa," Lizzie admitted. "Not when I stop to realize how grateful I am that God gave us Pa for as long as He did."

"Content," Jem added. "Not wantin' more, nor wishin' for less."

"Our secret to happiness," Lizzie whispered. "And even though my heart still feels like it's breakin' . . . I am, Jem. I'm happy, indeed, and content."

chapter
6

FANNY, with her days suddenly empty, graciously accepted a decrepit buggy that Jeremiah acquired in a zealous trade for some mules.

The conveyance allowed her to go visiting when Rory hitched Will's gentle sorrel mare to the sagging buggy, leaving her son the farm wagon to use with the workhorses around the acreage while she was off visiting.

A once-busy woman with a flock of visitors arriving on her doorstep, Fanchon Preston now had the leisure to return calls around the neighborhood. With her good humor and willingness to lend a capable hand to tasks, the widow was a welcome arrival at many a Salt Creek farmstead.

It became Fanny's mission in life to call on shut-ins, check on those who had no family close by and invite them to go to church services. She helped young matrons with their endless work and kept children occupied so their mothers could enjoy moments of respite from their endless duty. Her homemade candies and confections that she took along to give to those she visited were the talk of the area.

Early September coasted by. The first of October arrived in a blaze of color.

By mid-October the area had experienced its first frost.

"Br—r! Winter's in the air," Fanny announced later that same afternoon as she handed Jem the reins to the carriage.

"After the hot spell we suffered through this summer right before Will died," Jem said, "I'm one fellow who's looking forward to cool weather. So are my mules, I reckon."

Fanny gave a sudden gasp. "That reminds me! Speakin' o' mules, I heard tell that according to Lem Gartner mules are on the way out. Horses too! Lem lost a few horses this summer, and it put him behind in gettin' his crops in."

"That's happened to many a neighbor. Lizzie and I got off easy just losin' Harmon's old horse."

"Well, Lem Gartner vows it won't happen to him again, because he's about to take delivery of some newfangled whatchamacallit that'll make horses 'n' mules a thing of the past. He says it'll get here any day now—then horses will be on the way out. It'll be delivered by the Illinois Central Railroad at the freight depot. And I expect he'll drive it on home from there. He claims farmers will turn out in droves to get shed of their horses and mules and apply the money from the sale of their critters toward the purchase price of newfangled machines like the one he's got on order."

Jem gave an amused laugh. "I wouldn't hold my breath waiting on that prediction to come true, Mama."

"My! That's some boast on Lem's part!" Lizzie declared.

Fanny settled back in her kitchen chair. "Well, sure as God made little green apples, Lemont's gettin' him one o' 'em. I don't know exactly how they work, but neighbors are sayin' that it functions along the lines of building a fire—good and hot—stoking it like the pits of hell, then letting that iron beast het up a good head of steam to make it work. Anyway, iffen you keep that iron monster watered and feed the fire, that steam engine will work harder, faster, and longer than a half a dozen good horses."

"That may be," Jem said. "But it doesn't appeal to me."

"It sure enough appeals to Lem. He says that it won't have to stop to rest. And Lem vows that if we have a summer as hot as this past one's been, he won't have his iron beast dyin' on him. He says that you boys can keep your horses and feed your stubborn mules. He maintains that while you're rubbing down lathered beasts—he'll be sitting up high on that machine of his, just a-rootie-tootin' along—come what may. And he'll be puttin' his feet up and kickin' back in his rockin' chair, done with his day's labors while you boys are jus' getting started!"

"That's quite a claim," Jem said.

"And Lemont Gartner's been known to stretch the truth a bit farther than it was ever meant to extend," Lizzie added.

"Lem's right confident about it," Fanny went on. "And thoughtful, too, I must say, because he's already given his word that if we've another blistering summer, after he's attended to his farmin', he'll go around and lend a hand to all the neighbors."

"Lemont is a nice man," Lizzie mused. "Different. But nice. A wonder that he never took a wife. . . . He's a generous bloke, and easy to like."

"Nevertheless, I'll have to see his claims borne out for me to believe 'em," Fanny admitted, "but we're all going to get a chance to witness Lem's steam engine in action. He's going to thresh some wheat to prove to the menfolk who are doubting him just how slick that newfangled contraption works."

Jem wasn't convinced.

"I don't hold much faith in some puffing, huffing, snorting ol' machine," he derided. "A man can't make friends with a machine like he can a critter. Evenings when I've been so weary I could hardly put one foot ahead of the other as I head up the hill out of the bottomland to the cabin where I know

Lizzie 'n' the young'uns are waiting, old Mavis, or Birdie, they understand. One of those mules like as not'll nuzzle my back, walkin' close, just like she's kindly urging me up to the house where the family and a hot meal are waitin'. I dare anyone to suggest that a snortin' machine can be as considerate and concerned."

"You're as stubborn as your mules, dear," Lizzie retorted.

"Well, I, for one, am going to show up to witness such a sight," Fanny assured. "Lem says everyone's invited. We might even plan a potluck social to commemorate the occasion."

"That's a splendid idea," Lizzie said.

"We'll have to go check out this competition of ours, Liz, that Mama says is going to put me out of the mule-skinning, mule-selling business. Just tell us when Lem's holding his exposition, and we'll show up with bells on."

Cold weather landed with a vengeance the day of the exposition, but as the sun lifted overhead it burned off the frost and created a balmy day. Farm families packed their wagons and bundled in for the jouncing ride over the rough trails. A steady stream of conveyances wound up and down the hilly trails leading to Lemont Gartner's homestead.

The stout bachelor stood at the end of the lane, smiling wide. Neighbors milled around but seemed hesitant about approaching the gleaming iron monster. Lem—a jovial, rotund, prideful owner capered around it, secure in the miraculous capabilities of his prized acquisition.

"Step right up and look it over good, folks! It may be the first—but it won't be the last steam engine in these parts," he predicted. "You're seein' the future—tomorrow's modern farming machine *today*! You boys don't have to buy a pig in a poke. No-sirree! Try out my machine—and then mortgage the farm—and buy one for your very own!"

Lem mounted the machine and then sat in quiet pride as the men reached out, touching a bolt as they might have fingered a fetlock to insure a horse's soundness, or palpated a horse's chest to ascertain strength and stamina.

Lem oversaw the fueling of the machine. Bucket after bucket made its way from the cistern into the reservoir on the machine. Children scampered around for kindling, twigs, and raked-together straw and dead grass to feed the flames that Lemont ignited in the iron fire box.

Slowly, steadily the heat arose. When the steam pressure built, Lem yanked a cord, and the escaping force of the vapor caused a whistle to scream.

Women covered their ears, squealed in alarm, and pinched their eyes shut as crying, or giggling, young'uns clung to their skirts.

Putting the black, gleaming hulk into gear, Lem sat tall behind the controls and watched carefully as its vicious, spiked wheels gnawed into the ground, chewed over the terrain, and approached a huge pile of mounded wheat awaiting the threshing machine's digestion.

The men, interested and enthused, eager to take part in the exposition, jauntily followed after Lem in his miracle machine. They were ready to assist as he would ask of them in his preparations for the show. At his command the neighbors rushed around, realigning the wheels, adjusting the pulley, attaching the heavy belt that hooked the steam engine's power to throw into motion the rattling, clacking, thundering threshing machine that shook and shimmied as it performed its frenzied task.

Lem inched the massive machine back, gauging the tension of the softly slapping belt that grew evermore taut as the pulley spun faster until soon it was a whirling orb of steel. The supple belt that had lazily slapped with the first rhythms rat-a-tatted as the momentum increased until it whistled, slicing through the air, almost defying the eye to keep up with its motion.

The engine roared as the inferno blazed, shooting sparks and smoke up the chunky metal chimney. As if to draw attention—or create the noise of celebration—Lem pulled the cord again, cleaving the air with the moaning whistle that signaled that the beast was satiated and ready to work!

The audience of simple farmers was awed.

The wheat once piled high soon sank to a vanishing depth as sweating farmers fed the thresher.

"How many mules does it take to buy that steam engine, Lem?"

"More'n you've got, Jeremiah, my lad!" Lemont replied, and tossed Lizzie a laughing wink.

"Well, being as you've got that monster you're so fond of, might it be that you'll have mules you'd be in the market to sell?"

"I'm glad you asked! It so happens to be that I possess four of the dratted, accursed beasts, all o' them too confounded ornery to die in the summer's heat! Three of the mules I will sell to you, Jeremiah Stone. And the fourth—I'll make you a gift of that devil—as it will spare me the expense of producing a bullet with which to place a fatal slug between his obnoxious eyes!"

"Aw, Lem, we all know how you feel about mules," Jeremiah said. "Surely there's some good to be found in that flea-bitten jack."

Lem shook his head. He spat on the ground for emphasis. "That malevolent jack's different, Jem. I loathe the very sight of the stupid, stubborn brute! He's cause enough to make any mortal ripe to part with most of his life savings to buy a beast of iron." He laid a gentle hand on the rumbling machine. "A

84

metal beast who'll work for water 'n' fuel and not plot evil in his idle moments."

"If you wish to rid yourself of the mules, let's make a deal, Lem. Give me a price."

"Make me an offer."

And so the dickering began.

"I accept your terms, Jem," Lemont said. "And I'll throw in the jack for naught—just as I said. If there's any mule skinner who can make that beast pay attention, you're the bloke!"

"I've never met a mule I couldn't like," Jem said.

Lemont grinned and accepted Jem's handshake to seal the deal. "And, my lad, I don't recollect ever meeting one of the long-eared, short-tailed devils that I didn't eventually have good reason to despise!"

Jem took out his wallet and tendered a number of worn greenbacks and a precious gold coin.

With thanks Lemont pocketed the money.

"I'll bring the mules to your farm, 'n' the bill o' sale, as well. Unless you're wantin' me to prepare the papers now?"

Jem shook his head. "You're a man of your word, as I am."

As Lemont retreated to the controls of his marvelous machine, men clustered around Jeremiah, impressed with his deal for the mules that ended with a fair price for both buyer and seller.

"Lem's wrong," an area man said. "There'll still be a need for mules and horses."

"I'll keep mine around for sentimental reasons if for none other," someone else spoke up.

"Well, you boys can have your obstreperous critters," said another as he chewed on a blade of wheat straw. "If I had the money I'd be followin' Lemont's suit."

"Me too. My pappy hated mules, although he dearly loved

his horses. No man could've run fast enough to have caught Pa to give him a mule."

"To hate mules like that he must've owned some once, 'n' took the cure like I did. I won't have one of the raucous beasts on my eighty acres."

"Pa got turned against mules when he was a lad," the man replied, and he gave a helpless chuckle.

The neighbor man's eyebrow flicked up, silently encouraging him to continue with the story.

"Pappy was just a young pup," the fellow continued. "He and his folks lived over in Missouri at the time. That's real mule country, y'know. Well, my granddaddy sent my pa, who was pro'bly ten or eleven at the time, into town with a load of grain on a wagon. And he told him to settle up in town and use the money to buy supplies for the fam'bly."

The men nodded as they listened. They had all known similar experiences.

"So Pa hitched up the mule, the biggest, strongest one that Granddaddy had, to hear him tell it when I was growin' up. He got that ol' mule to town, he went by the grain depot, the wagon was unloaded, the deal was executed, and Pa went to the general store and took out the earnings in trade. He got everything on Grandmammy's list and stowed it in that big ol' wagon."

The farmer barely contained a smile as he adjusted his hat.

"Now my pappy was just a boy. And it was his first time to town all alone. So, he done what a boy'll do, and he had to show off for whoever was watching. He wanted the citizens in that fine town to take notice that he was man enough to be trusted to take his pa's best mule to town and do the fam'bly trading."

The men who comprised his audience nodded. Most of

them knew just the exact same heady experience the story-teller's pa had entertained on that hallmark day.

"Well, Pa admitted that he drove up and down the street, showin' off that fine mule, tippin' his hat to all the ladies, saying 'Howdy!' and 'Good day!' to all the gentlemen."

"And probably givin' shy smiles to the girls," a Salt Creek neighbor interjected.

"Right you are!" the speaker agreed. "That's exactly what he did. From the sounds of it, Pa took that mule up and down every street and avenue in the town, and he tarried to the point where that ol' mule was goin' to have to hurry if they were going to get home in time. They set out for Grandpappy's farm, and because that mule was plumb tuckered out by then, he wasn't in the notion to hurry every chance he got. Just as you'd expect, my pa started thinking about the scolding he might get for bein' a tad irresponsible, so he larruped the mule a time or two—trying to encourage him to quicken his pace."

"I'll wager that was a mistake!" a man said and guffawed.

"It sure was! 'Stead of speeding up, that ol' mule cocked back his ears and made it a point to actually slow down. Fact is, he not only slowed down—with another few minutes he'd come to a dead stop."

A chorus of groans arose from those gathered.

"I've had that happen—and there are few things so infuriating. What'd your pa do then?"

"What any average bloke would've. He laid on the mule a bit heavier with the whippin' stick. But that only made the critter all the more obstinate. He cocked his hind leg, rested on his hooftip like he was planning on takin' his ease for the rest of the day. He laid back his ears and half-closed his eyes. No matter what Pa done to him, that mule didn't so much as flick a hair in acknowledgment."

"And meanwhile, time was tickin' on!"

"It sure was, and Pappy was about ready to cry, I expect, and he was up hauling on the mule's harness, encouraging him to get moving. But you know how a mule is. Why, when a jack decides he's tired and has worked enough, he ain't movin' a muscle 'til he decides that he's sufficiently rested. And Pa didn't have the time to waste."

"I've seen mule skinners can't get a stubborn jack or jenny to move. No way would a mere lad accomplish it."

"Oh, but Pa did," the man exclaimed and began to laugh. "My pappy is a pretty smart fellow, and obviously he was even as a young'un. My Grandmammy had had Pa pick up some kitchen matches amongst the household notions she was needin'. And it seems that my Grandpappy, when the young'uns wasn't helping out as much as he felt they should, would say something like, 'Y'all want me to light a fire under you to get ya goin'?' So my pa decides that he'll light a fire under the mule. Pa raked together a bit of dried grass from the roadway, scratched around until he located bits of kindling, and he hunkered down beside that mule and he made a neat little nest of kindling on the ground beneath that mule's belly, and presently he touched one of Grandmammy's kitchen matches to it, and made the nicest little blaze you ever did see."

"Bet that got the mule's attention!"

"It sure enough did. That ol' mule opened his eyes wide, jerked his head up, twitched his tail, and he stepped right lively as he pranced on over that fire and got movin' again. Pappy was feelin' almost overwhelmed with relief as he clambered up into the wagon seat and clutched up the reins, intent on bein' on his way. Pa had pulled a pretty smart maneuver to get the mule puttin' one foot ahead of the other again, but it didn't last for long. It turns out that the mule had out-thought my pappy, for the mule moved ahead *just enough* so that it parked the wagon loaded with all the staples and supplies, right over that dandy little blaze that my pappy'd built."

Another chorus of groans went up.

"Grandpappy always pitched the underside of his wagons to help make 'em waterproof to prevent wood rot, and that pine pitch caught on fire quick as a wink. Pa must've been almost in tears as he saw flames lickin' up. He hied onto the wagon and began tossin' purchases off on the roadbed. It almost mortally pained him to have to unhitch that mule. But he knew he was in for trouble enough, arranging to cause Grandpappy's wagon to burn, 'thout also causin' the destruction of his best mule. About that time a bloke came along and he helped my pappy put out the fire and salvage a bit of the wagon's framework. They hitched it to his wagon, loaded Pa's purchases into the fellow's empty wagon, and he hauled Pa and his burdens home, laughin' all the way every time he thought of what a sight he'd come upon. Meanwhile, I expect my pa was ready to bawl at the prospect of what awaited him when he got home."

"Did he really get a lickin' when he got home?" a neighbor asked.

"He sure anticipated one," the storyteller said. "But he was surprised. Grandpappy, I guess, figured Pa had suffered enough. He gave him a stiff talking to, and told him to let it be a lesson about mules and showin' off for the world."

"Valuable lessons, both."

"Pa learned 'em, I reckon, but he also gained knowledge to start despisin' mules. He refused to ever own one or work one."

"He ain't the only one. My pappy worked to put in the Illinois Central Rail bed some years back. They used mules 'n' tumble-bugs to haul up sufficient dirt to mound it up for layin' of the rails. The contractors bought up, or leased, mules when they'd pass through an area, 'n' my pa was one of the 'skinners. A farmer saw his opportunity, and he sold the railroad a mule that no one else would've given more than a bullet between his eyes. One look at that mule, and Pa knew what was in store."

"How so?"

The farmer made a slashing gesture from the corner of his mouth running back to his ears.

"Because, boys, that jack's face was ripped—*ripped*—from the corner of his mouth clean back to his jaw! The jack's face was jagged and scarred. And it takes a powerful vicious bit to rip through an animal's hide from a 'skinner sawin' on the reins. And it takes a powerful vicious animal to require one such tack."

Quickly the story was told. The mule skinners working for the railroad endured that beast, groaning each time they drew the lot that required them to work that particular beast for the day.

"One day that mule went plumb loco. Even with a bicycle bit in his mouth to try to control him, there was no stopping him. He took off across the countryside, goin' like ninety, and that tumble-bug was bouncing behind him. He warn't the smartest mule in the world, leastways, not like some of 'em, because he didn't have the intelligence to know when he'd had enough. He dropped dead in the railbed—a heart attack, most likely—and they unhitched him, levered the tumble bug away, and they simply covered that beast up with dirt and continued on. My pappy said it was a day he gave thanks to the Lord that the mule died before he could kill a man."

"That's true enough."

"Pa showed me that section of railbed," he finished.

"Pointed out just exactly where that ol' mule is laying beneath the sod. I think of it every time I go by. . . ."

"Mules can be dangerous devils," another took up the conversation. "I've heard tell that you'd better be nice to 'em even if you hate 'em with a passion, because it's claimed that a mule doesn't ever forget. Treat him bad—and he'll lay for you—try to kill you, even, iffen he can. But treat him kind, and that mule will do his all for ya."

"That's how I see it," Jeremiah said. "I've treated my mules well and they've accorded me the same kind of behavior. I handle 'em as if they're family. In many ways they are . . . Just as human beings will blossom under kindness, and even the hardest heart can eventually be softened with gentle, kind behavior, and expressions of carin' love, I believe the same is possible with mules."

"There are those who, respectin' you as they do, Jeremiah Stone, would, at hearin' that kind o' talk, label you a fool."

Jem gave a good laugh. "Right you are—with my Lizzie at the head of the list!"

"Ready to go, boys?" Lemont bellowed in a hearty tone as he drew his iron beast toward the cluster of neighbors who were milling around, chatting.

"I've got a horse that can count," a farmer razzed Lemont, cupping his hands around his mouth so the proud host could hear him. "Anything else that your fancy machine can do but thresh?"

"My steam engine can do more than power the threshin' machine. I'll guarantee that it can do about anything that a horse or mule can do. You boys step lively over to the log pile to help, 'n' I'll show you!"

Lemont gingerly drove the cumbersome machine to a nearby clearing at the edge of the woods where a buzz-saw frame was silhouetted against the timber, secured to the ground by iron pegs. Nearby was a pile of logs and poles that had seasoned over the summer and awaited being lopped into stove lengths.

Men limbered up the sawtable, pushing it back and forth a few times in front of the motionless blade, contenting themselves of its agility. "Fire away!" Lem cheered the flurry of children.

Familiar this time, the sweaty, eager men linked the engine to the sawmill. Lem backed the machine into the perfect position. The pulley whirled. The belt's tension tightened after a farmer looped it into contact with the sawmill. Lem set the brake. He threw a gear. The belt leaped.

The first revolution of the saw blade twirled slowly. Faster and faster it spun until soon it was a blur as it reached peak momentum. The razor sharp edge sliced the air emitting a high, eerie scream. Men cheered. They grinned and shook their heads when they considered the potent strength and speed of the buzz saw and compared it to the slow, tedious, back-breaking alternative of an ax, or a sawbuck and crosscut.

With a yell they hefted an oak log.

Issuing a high whine the twirling blade nosed into the rough log. The saw growled, grumbled, complained, but relentlessly gnawed on until it exited the other side with a victorious shriek when the stove length of firewood sheered off, hitting the cold ground with a muffled thud.

The men worked on. Back, forth. Back, forth. The saw platform supporting the log rocked rhythmically beneath the men's sure grip.

Rumble, growl, scream. Rumble, growl, scream.

Without halting to rest, the whirling blade sliced through the logs as fast as the men could carry them from the pile. Lem beamed from his place astride his willing beast.

Men were engaged in their unaccustomed manner of work,

so different from the slow-paced methods. Women, talking loudly and shrilly to be heard above the tremendous din, marveled at the expensive machine's ability and how it might contribute to spare their husbands from physical hardship and deterioration of health.

Children, shrieking and laughing, had lost all fear of the machine.

"Oh, *no!*"

A young mother's horrified cry soared above then blended in with the saw's scream when she turned to discover her toddler no longer clinging to her skirts, but instead, tottering toward the lethal blade that spun, glinting beneath the autumn sun.

The men, working as one with the machine, adopting its special rhythm, failed to see the child's approach. The mother's screams were blotted from their hearing by the saw's banshee howl and the steam engine's heated rumble.

Lem glanced down and saw too late. The steam engine slackened as he slammed it from gear, idling the engine. But the belt and blade spun on, driven by momentum the machine already possessed.

The tot's mother stood rooted in horror, incapable of movement as her face drained milky white from terror, and she closed her eyes, swooning, unable to view the inevitable.

When Lem shut down the engine, puzzled, the men glanced up, inquiringly.

Their eyes were yanked to the approaching child, but they were on the wrong side of the belt to intercept his path. They screamed and wildly gestured for the child to get away.

Confused, he tottered and stumbled. As he arose, righting himself, his small head came perilously close to the twirling blade.

Fanny Preston, reacting from years of experience, seemed

to roll over the ground, a squat, rotund bundle of wool shawl and full calico skirt. Her tiny feet pittered over the turf carrying her to the child.

The community heaved a collective sigh of relief.

In the precious seconds that elapsed, the blade continued to sing its sinister song.

A cry of triumph arose as Fanny snatched the child from harm's way. She turned on her heel, inches short of the gradually slowing blade.

A random gust of wind—a breeze all but unnoticed by them that day as accustomed as they were to its constant activity—plucked at Fanny's voluminous dress of stout, almost new fabric.

The yards of material in her skirt billowed, and almost faster than the eye could detect, were snagged by the saw teeth and snarled tight, the force yanking her up close.

With a desperate, startled cry she flung the child from her as she toppled around, a moment before the force would've pitched the tot up into the air to land on the jagged blade as he fell back to the earth.

Fanny was yanked upright, toppled, then was dashed to the ground headfirst. In the moment it took to occur, her eyes widened as she looked out over her friends and neighbors, recorded shock, disbelief, then her eyes closed in perfect knowledge and acceptance of what was happening.

There was a sickening thud, a dull snap, and Fanny was presented instantaneous death, her neck broken as she was dashed to the ground, and the blade released its sharp-toothed grip on her ripped skirt.

Those present sobbed their despair at her grisly leaving. Lem—all of them—were weeping and keening as it seemed to take an eternity for the belt to slow and flop from the pulley, curling back to snake over Fanny's still form.

With a terrible, baying cry, Lizzie stumbled toward her mother, shaking away the touch of those who would restrain her.

"Mama, Mama!" she bawled as her tears fell from her cheeks to land on Fanny's slack face.

Lizzie clutched Fanny Preston's buxom form to her, rocking her back and forth as tears flooded over her cheeks and she cradled her mother's lifeless form.

A cry, echoing Lizzie's, tore from Rory. When word reached him of the tragic, freak accident, he had reacted with disbelief.

But the vision of his grieving sister dashed him with icy reality, and then it evolved to become fiery rage that left him momentarily incapable of speech as boiling thoughts scalded his mind.

With the aid of a walking stick, he stumped his way to the center of the crowd. Possessed, consumed by grief and throbbing rage, Rory Preston stood over his mother's lifeless body and cursed God.

Only when he was spent and the wellspring of his fury had run dry, did he halt and settle for angrily glaring at neighbors.

"And don't tell me that I'm wrong in feeling as I do—and saying what I have. Spare your breath spouting Scripture at me! Console yourselves, if you will, contenting yourselves that it's God's will." He gave a bitter, cold laugh. "I know that cruel fact well, myself, for what you witness is an atrocity that the Lord most definitely has allowed to befall my mother! And why, I ask you?"

He looked down at Fanny, seemed about to burst into wretched tears, then his chin grew rigid and he shook his head sickly.

"She deserved better than God ever gave her!" Rory insisted, his voice cracking. "She was a good woman, a righteous person, and He handed her a humiliating death—a broken neck, thrashed to death in front of her helpless family and friends. The supposed mercy of such a God disgusts me!"

The crowd gasped. They whirled to stare at one another, but no one present knew quite what to say in the face of such blasphemy, because to a one they all felt that Fanny, dear soul that she was, had died in a horrible way, not in a manner they'd have selected for a favorite in the community

Lizzie struggled to her feet. She faced Rory over their mother's lifeless form. She started to reach out, to slap him a stinging blow across his cheek. But she checked the motion and her hand dropped to her side.

Tears, gleaming like diamonds in the sunlight, rolled down her cheeks. She spoke only to her brother, although all gathered there could hear.

"God Almighty presented His Son a death no better, Rory Preston. He suffered a humiliating, painful, public death that was much, much worse! Mama died quickly and without pain, savin' the life of a little boy she'd want to enable to live even if it meant departin' herself!"

"Shut up, Lizzie!" Rory thundered indignantly. "Blame fool!"

She gave him a withering glance that stilled his protests.

"Mama died in the way she lived: helpin' and servin' others. And I pray her example not be lost on you forever, Rory. . . ."

Jeremiah went to Rory. He put his arm around the heartbroken, furious young man. He led him away as neighbors looked on, aghast.

"You're Will and Fanny Preston's son," Lizzie screamed after her brother. "For the love of God—start acting like it— or I'll thrash you like the upstart, opinionated brat you are!"

Rory, rising to his sister's bait, as he had since they were children, challengingly turned back toward her, but Jem curtly jerked him around and onward as the crowd parted to allow them passage.

Alton, taking control of the situation as Jem led Rory away, dispersed the crowd, but detained a few trusted neighbors to help with the reverent removal of Fanny's body and its transport home.

Lizzie had never known such grief as when she bathed her mother's body and prepared it for burial, placing it in the new box scarcely completed by Jeremiah, but as precise and perfect as the caskets of Will Preston's creation.

The night and day passed in a numbing blur of faces, words, responses.

Fanny was buried in the drenching rain as if the very heavens wept to mourn her passing. Then it was over.

Four days later, Lem Gartner, who'd earlier sent word that he'd bring the mules at Jem's convenience, delivered the beasts.

Lem hung his head. "I meant what I said, Jeremiah. In light of what's happened, you needn't feel bound by our agreement."

"It wasn't your fault, Lemont. You adored Fanny as did everyone in the neighborhood. No hard feelings," Jeremiah assured him, although both of the men were painfully aware that Lizzie did not leave the shelter of her cabin to greet a guest.

"If you're sure," Lemont murmured, his tone uncertain.

"It's a deal," Jem affirmed. "I'm a man of my word, and I'm keepin' the bargain not to maintain my honor but in a desire to own these fine mules you're bent on relievin' yourself of, friend. You're sure you're satisfied with the amount? It seems a pittance."

"More than satisfied," Lem said. "I'd best be going." He

glanced at the cabin. Lem tipped his hat in that direction.
"Give your Missus my regards—'n' my regrets."

"I will," Jem promised.

"Lemont offered to free you from your agreement, didn't
he?" Lizzie asked in an accusing tone when Jem entered the
house.

"You read Lem's note the other day. You know that he
did."

"I wish you would have accepted his gesture!" Lizzie said
and banged her cast iron skillet onto the top of the range.

"I could've. But I didn't. Liz, I *want* those mules."

"Well, *I* don't!"

Lizzie turned, her face glaring, her features haggard with
grief, fatigue, and fear.

"Honey, be reasonable. Lemont had nothing—"

"Mules, mules, *mules!*" Lizzie exploded. "That's all I hear
out of you, Jeremiah Stone, and it's gettin' worse. The boys
are picking it up from you. Those vile beasts will be the death
of you or one of our young'uns some sad day. You all laugh
when they kick the slats out of the stalls in the barn. Well, I
cringe!"

"Oh, now sweetheart," Jem comforted.

Lizzie began to sob.

"You laugh over the outlandish mule stories farmers tell
and retell them yourself. Always, you're championing mules'
wisdom, recognizing their wiles, their stubborn wickedness.
You laugh—but inside—I cry with every repetition!"

"Liz, what's gotten into you?" Jem asked quietly.

Flustered, she was silently, mentally taking stock of herself
and the situation. She flung a wild gesture toward the barn
lot. She didn't really know. Just a feeling. A terrible,
foreboding, unidentifiable sensation of fear.

"That mule. That one right out there!" she cried for an

answer, rather than humiliate herself with an inability to explain and lay blame for her upsetting feelings.

Jem knew the destination of her gesture.

The maverick mule just delivered by Lemont Gartner cavorted and capered through the pasture, creating vicious havoc in plain sight through their kitchen window.

"Mules will be mules," Jem offered weakly.

Lizzie gave an angry bleat of disgust.

"That mule's the devil's own spawn, Jeremiah! Better that Lem would have given him a load of lead between the eyes then give him to you—and gift me with an unending burden of fear."

"You know nothing will happen to me unless God allows it," Jem said. "Please don't take on so, Lizzie. I'll work with the mule a week or two. If he shows no sign of change—I'll rid the world of him. And that's my solemn promise."

Lizzie curled a lip over the offer. "He'll not change."

"Now, you don't know that for sure," Jem pointed out.

"How can you believe so adamantly that he will?"

Jem captured an unwilling Lizzie in his embrace, holding her until he subdued her with his greater strength and his patient determination.

He laughed as her anger wilted and she held him tight, so very tight, as if she'd never let him go.

"*You* changed through the influence of my love, you proud, stubborn beauty. Perhaps the jack will, too."

"Oh, Jem," Lizzie wailed.

"Lizzie—be content—be happy. I'll try the mule and if he's as you say, rid us of him immediately."

Lizzie pried herself from his arms but then burrowed back into his embrace, more miserable without his arms around her than she'd been angered by his forceful but loving restraint.

"By then it may be too late," she warned in a numb, hollow

tone. And with the thought lodged solidly in her mind, she grew silent, fearful to speak, afraid to even think. . . .

A solid thud lashed the side of the barn. Jem whistled low. "That's a powerful fellow," he acknowledged, laughing.

Lizzie listened. And shuddered as a loathing chill pierced to the marrow when the sound came again. *THUD!*

chapter

7

"Yoo-hoo! Lester, Maylon, Thad!" Lizzie bawled at dawn.

"What, Mama?" came the sleepy response.

"Time to get up 'n' get ready for school."

A minute later, sleepy heads appeared and presently Lizzie's sons appeared in the kitchen and lined up to take their turns at the washstand in the corner of the room near the woodstove, where it was warm enough for wintery bathing.

"'Morning, boys," Lizzie said in a pleasant tone. A moment later, worry made her feel snappish, and she couldn't help greeting them with dire warnings.

A chorused, "'Mornin', Mama," was lost as Lizzie spoke on.

"If y'all go near the pasture, set so much as a toe behind the gate, and I vow 'n' declare that I'll skin your bony shanks the way your foolhardy pa's intent on skinnin' that stubborn, flea-bitten mule!"

Sighing wearily, Lizzie sank into a chair and took a sip of scalding coffee that seemed to revive her senses and filled her with a facsimile of calm.

"Boys, I'm sorry for ragin' at you like a shrew. That jack your pa got from Lemont Gartner's got me as nervous as a long-tailed tabby cat in a room full o' rockin' chairs."

"Pa says he's a mean 'un," Lester remarked as he scooped up his oatmeal that dripped with heavy cream and brown sugar.

"That he is," Lizzie sighed. "'N' even if it's evil of me to wish death to a creature, I sorely hope that mule's days are keenly numbered. Like your grandpapa Will used to say, 'Better to suffer death in the barn or pasture than to mourn loss of life among those residin' in the cabin.'"

Hours passed slowly as Lizzie found herself counting the days since the mule's arrival on their farm.

On Saturday Miss Abby and the Wheeler girls visited briefly with Lizzie while Alton viewed Jem's growing herd of mules.

"I see that jack Jeremiah acquired from Lemont Gartner is still in the pasture."

"Unfortunately," Lizzie sighed. "If wishes could make a beast vanish—that mule would've disappeared long ago."

"Jem hasn't given up on him yet?"

"No," Lizzie said shortly. "I don't know who's crazier—Jem or that loco mule. He declared that he'd give that jack two weeks to show a sign of change."

"That must seem like an eternity for you, Lizzie."

Lizzie's eyes filled with tears. "It is, Miss Abby. I scarcely dare turn my back or blink for fear that Harmony will slip away 'n' follow her pa to the pasture. Jem says the mule's got two weeks—no more. 'N' meanwhile, Jem turns a deaf ear to me while I remind him not to test the Lord, but instead rid the earth of that mule's presence the sooner the better."

Just then Jem and Alton entered the house.

"Son, I agree with Lizzie. That mule's a killer. I wouldn't have such a beast around my wife 'n' young'uns."

"See!" Lizzie cried, gloating, giving Alton a baldly grateful look. "Whyn't you do as your pa suggests?"

"Now, Liz," Jem said, "we've been through this time 'n' again, 'though that jack's only been on the farm nine days."

"'N' has he shown so much as a speck of change?"

"No . . . but I hate to kill the beast without keepin' my word—"

In anger Lizzie flung a dishtowel across the room. She leaped out of the chair.

"Then *load* the confounded gun, Jeremiah Stone," she squalled like a scalded cat, her eyes sparking, "and *I'll* do it!"

"Liz, let's not fight—"

"I'm not fighting," Lizzie said, and her voice quaked. "I'm just making my wishes clear. Jem, you have a responsibility to me 'n' the young'uns to keep us safe."

Jem flinched as if he'd been slapped. Alton coughed and cleared his throat.

"I'll end that mule's misery—'n' Lizzie's agony—'n' everyone else's for that matter, if you want me to, son. I'll be honest, Jem, we've all been worried. 'Twould have been better had Lem blasted the mule into the next county rather than gift you with his troubles."

"You're right, Pa." Jem squared his shoulders, as if to signal that it was settled. "I'll do it. He's my mule—the stubborn rascal—somehow I feel that I owe it to that jack to end his life myself and not pass the unpleasantness off to another."

Lizzie snorted. "I'd take delight in causin' that cocky, brazen, evil-hearted, simple-minded mule to breathe his last!" She paused for breath. "Mark my words—if that mule causes harm to befall you, or one of my children, I'll strangle the wretch with my bare hands!"

Jem laughed, but it sounded forced. He put his arm around Lizzie, and gave her a quick hug.

"Listen to Lizzie, Pa! It appears the wrong person may have been attemptin' to work with that mule. Maybe I should

103

put on Lizzie's apron 'n' tend the cabin while she talks sense into a crazy mule."

"I'm afeard that it ain't a jokin' matter, Jeremiah," Alton said, clamping Jem's shoulder. "C'mon, son. Let's you 'n' me go out and finish off that ornery old hayburner and provide Miss Lizzie with a peaceful night's sleep. I'm sure she could use one."

"Naw," Jem demurred, "morning's soon enough."

Jem reached for the coat he'd not long before found reason to remove. It seemed likely that he was wanting to escape Lizzie's worried, sullen presence, lightened only a bit with his promise that come the beginning of the next day, the mule's existence would cease.

Lizzie invited Miss Abby, Alton, and their girls to stay for supper, but the couple declined, expressing a wish to get home in time for Alton to attend to choring.

The atmosphere around the table was pleasant—more pleasant than it had seemed to be in weeks—and the children lingered, talking about their day at school as Jeremiah and Lizzie relished a second cup of coffee each.

The children helped Lizzie in the kitchen, then took turns bathing in the wash basin.

Lizzie gave Harmony a bath and tucked her into bed at the same time the boys climbed the ladder to the attic to retire. She went to the side door to toss her washwater into the back yard. Jem was seated in the darkness on a block of firewood that he hadn't yet had time to split for the stove.

"Thinkin'?" Lizzie asked.

"Uh-huh," Jem said.

Lizzie stood beside him and he slipped his arm around her hips and drew her close. She rested her hand on his strong shoulder and her heart felt overpowered by love.

Then, as she heard the ominous thuds and thumps from

behind the barn, which that fool mule seemed intent on tearing down splinter by splinter, a tendril of fear twined around her heart, the growth fanning out in shoots.

"Y—you *are* goin' to do away with that mule first thing in the mornin', ain't ya? Just like you said?"

"I told you that I would, Liz. . . ."

She patted his shoulder. "You're a man of your word. It's good as done."

The twilight silence an of Indian summer eve enveloped them. They talked on a long time as they gazed at the stars and admired the huge silvery moon that slanted in a direct path across the heavens as it rose. Eventually the silence was shattered by Harmony's cry.

"I'll go see what's the matter with the Harmony," Lizzie said, arising. She halted. "Jem?"

"Yes?"

"Jeremiah, I love you! I love you so much that . . . that . . . it's hurtful. It's such a sweet pain in my heart!"

"Oh, Liz," he whispered. "I love you too. Love you more than my own life. I adore you, sassy 'n' headstrong as you are!"

Lizzie gave a rueful laugh, unable to quite tear herself away, even though Harmony panted between angry cries.

"Sometimes you make me mad as blue blazes, and rile me with what seems foolishness and irritation. I don't mean to get sharp and testy with you sometimes. I only get that way from lovin' you so much that it's a raw fear somethin' will happen."

Jem arose. "You'd best go see about our li'l one, woman," he reminded, "'stead o' standin' out under the moonlight sparkin' with a fellow that loves you. And I do, Lizzie girl. I love you so much, why, I allow that I love you more'n I do my mules!"

Lizzie giggled, but was pleased. "You heartless tease. More'n your mules. Harumph!"

"Harmony needs you, honey," Jem said to a chuckling Liz. "It sounds like she's having a bad dream."

"I'm going in right now," she said. "Will you be in soon?"

"I'll only be a little while longer, Liz."

Content, Lizzie entered the cabin to tend to Harmony, who clung to her mother, requiring Lizzie to stay with her, crooning and offering comfort for long minutes.

When Lizzie went inside their home, Jeremiah impulsively jumped up. Rapidly but noiselessly, he entered the cabin and crossed to the gunrack over the mantel and hefted down his double-barreled shotgun from its customary resting place.

He slipped two slugs into the chambers, then silently exited the cabin and made his way through the serenity to face his destiny in the mule pasture. Jem lounged against the barn, thinking, remembering.

Gradually his eyes adjusted to the dim light.

The silvery sheen of light cast off by the moon silhouetted familiar landmarks and outlined the motions of the beasts as they grazed in the night.

Jem saw the maverick mule.

He watched him. He pitied him. But he knew that such an evil, unrepentant beast could not be allowed to live that another—his precious Lizzie, or his beloved children—might accidentally die through his own mulish stubbornness about the jack.

Jem let himself into the pasture and carefully secured the gate after himself. His footsteps were muffled by the dewy grass.

He shivered from the dampness in the air and hurried a bit as he anticipated the warmth of the cabin and the wife who awaited him.

Lizzie was right about the mule, Jeremiah realized. But then, little-educated-but-full-of-horse-sense Lizzie was right about a lot of things. She was a headstrong gal but one with a strong head about right and wrong.

Jem crept near the mule. It seemed to give no hint that it was aware of his presence, although Jem knew that the mule couldn't help but catch his scent.

The moon passed behind some clouds that scudded across the sky. Jem squinted down the length of the barrels. The moon peeped out again, making a ray of white run the straight length of the blue-black barrels. Just as he got the mule perfectly in his sights and was about to press off a fatal shot, a whimsical cloud seemed to dance across the path of the moon, halving the light.

For a moment it was as if the world were plunged into darkness save for the twinkling stars that offered little assistance for the task he faced that gloomy night.

Jem exhaled, waiting patiently, for the clouds to move on and reveal the full moon once more. Around him he heard the milling of the mules, but he dared not talk to those who would welcome his presence there, for fear of alerting the one he parried with in a most dangerous duel. A cloud flitted. Light slashed. Jem squinted down the barrel, the maple stock hard against his cheekbone. His arms ached from holding the gun in position when he'd rather be holding his Lizzie.

"Jem!" He heard Lizzie's call in the night. But he dared not answer. "Jem!"

He was about to turn away, to postpone the task until morning as he'd stated. But he wanted to complete the unpleasant labor that they could freely turn their minds and hearts to happier thoughts without the specter of the vicious jack clouding their contentment for even a night.

He waited . . . waited. . . .

He was tempted to blast off the shots when the light erupted for a taunting moment. But he forced patience in himself. If he merely nicked the jack, injured and enraged, there was no telling what damage the mule would do to the jennies and mares in the pasture.

It was a requisite that he shoot with surety.

As he waited, gooseflesh tingled over Jem's arms. Nonsensical as he thought it, he had the eerie sensation as if the mule *was* evil, and *was* matching wits with him, *was* using the darkness just as Jeremiah desperately awaited the light.

To get off better shots, Jeremiah crept ahead, seeking his footing with nudging toes as he gained inch by precious inch on the mule.

A breeze whispered through the woods nearby, shaking the branches of the trees, creating a dry clatter and crackle with the dying leaves that had yet to fall. Nearby an owl screeched, the sound almost unnerving Jem, even though he was quite unafraid in the night.

"Please, God!" Jem whispered, as he waited for the clouds to lift and the light to appear.

Then, almost immediately, it did.

His finger caressed the triggers.

Jem anticipated the explosions as he faced the mule—the jack much closer than he'd remembered—his eyes seeming to flame with a fiery glare. Squeezing tightly, steadily, Jeremiah moved the triggers and expected the thundering report at any instant.

The explosion arrived, brilliant fire flaming from the tip of the barrel.

But at the moment of the explosion and before he could squeeze off a second shot, the outburst seared from his nose to his brain, with white-hot fire and a roaring that spread out to fill his head, then his entire being.

Another explosion of a powerful hoof flipped Jem about like a rag doll, and destroyed his thoughts almost as they were formed.

Another!

Then another!

And Jeremiah Stone crumpled in the pasture and felt and thought no more. . . .

At the cabin, Lizzie wrapped a shawl around her. The night wasn't that chilly—but the apprehension she felt made her grow cold. She returned to the side door. Jem wasn't seated on the chunk of oak where she had left him.

"Jem!" She went to the front yard. "*Jem!*" she cried again, but all to no avail.

Lizzie's fear quickly grew to become nervous anger. She leaned against the gate, pretending a boldness she didn't really feel.

"Jem!" she bawled into the night.

No answer.

"I know you're out there," she muttered under her breath, "'n' if you jump out and play bogeyman at me, scarin' me half to death, I swear I'm never goin' to speak to you again as long as I live, 'n' see how you like that!" she whispered hotly. "*JEM!*"

Lizzie got no answer. She'd hoped for a guffaw that'd give away his hiding place. When silence reigned, without Jem emerging from the shadows to razz her and hug her tight, laughing in her ear as he clucked away her anger, terror worked a frozen path to her very soul.

She stood rigid, frozen, not knowing which way to turn, where to search in the consuming darkness.

And, as she frightened herself with the unspeakable possibilities, it was easier to do nothing than stumble about in the darkness and risk finding a sight that she'd wish with all her heart she would never have to see.

In the few moments when she found herself incapable of action, her mind seemed to fling her thoughts into a thousand directions at once. Then haunted by the darkness and the horrible screech of an owl nearby that sent her blood like ice water through her veins, Lizzie dashed into the house.

Her eyes were drawn to the gun rack.

Jeremiah's double-barreled shotgun was gone!

Why hadn't she seen it? She felt almost weak with relief. She hastily pictured Jem, alive, well, regretfully admonishing the maverick mule for his malicious ways, then, raising the gun, apologizing, even as he—

BANG!

The shot Lizzie had anticipated arrived. She awaited the second loud report. It never came. Nor did the inhumane shriek of the dying jack. It must have been a clean shot, she contented herself. Right between the eyes.

Seconds passed by like minutes, minutes like hours.

There was no more patience to be found in her. Lizzie stepped outside and screamed for Jem.

Surely, surely, he'd answer her, bellow at her that he was all right, merely tending to the disposal of the dead jack before he came in to retire for the night. But her frantic cries spookily echoed back at her as Jeremiah failed to call out to her.

Lizzie's screams brought the frightened boys bounding down the attic ladder.

"Ma, what is it? Mama, what's going on?" they cried.

"Your papa . . ." was all she could say. "He's out in the pasture, and—"

Then she began to sob.

White-faced, their features pinched with fear, they lit the

lanterns and accompanied their quaking mother to the mule pasture.

"Oh dear God in heaven, no! I can't stand it. No! Oh, God, don't let Jem be dead!" Lizzie whimpered.

"Ma, is he dead?" Thad asked, beginning to cry harder. Finally they found him. They clustered around as Lester held the coal oil lantern aloft. The three boys looked down at Jeremiah, bloody, still. Tears dripping from her cheeks, Lizzie rolled Jem over. He emitted a low groan.

"Oh, thank the Lord! There's still life in his body," she said, crying harder but this time with relief.

Lizzie flung herself across his prostrate form, sobbing and praying. Her ear on his chest detected a heartbeat, different from her own that raced.

Snorting, braying, a minute later the maverick mule circled back intent on launching another attack.

But Mavis, Jem's docile, loving old jenny, and one he'd vowed never to sell, sniffed the air, and trotted over, flapping her long ears in alarm. She placed herself between the loco jack and the defenseless mother and her three young.

"He's alive, boys!" Lizzie panted. "We've got to move him from the pasture. Oh, God in heaven, give us the strength!"

They wallowed Jem off the ground, tripping, stumbling as they struggled to move him to a place of safety.

Mavis took vicious blows on her body, and the loyal old jenny bit and kicked at the jack in return. Lizzie wept when she saw the old mule's valiant efforts. Mavis backed up, fighting for her ground before the much larger jack forced her to give it up.

Lizzie and her sons jounced Jem through the gate opening, regretful that there was no other choice but to handle him so roughly in their desperate haste.

His teeth chattering with fright, Lester slammed the gate

shut so fast he caught Mavis's tail in it. As he opened the gate
to free her, Maylon grasped the jenny's halter and jerked her
from the pasture and the jack's continued abuse.

"Thank God you thought fast, Maylon, and brought Mavis
out," Lizzie said. "We need her."

"'N' that jack would've killed her," he said quietly.

"Lester, be a good boy," Lizzie said. "As soon as we get
your pa into the house, you ride as hard and fast as you can
for Uncle Rory. Have him send for the doctor. No," Lizzie
changed her mind. "Have him come to help me. No," she
changed her mind again. "Oh, just go do something. Get
somebody! Please!"

The boys and Lizzie wrestled Jem's limp form into the
cabin and on beyond to the bedroom.

Lester didn't even glance back. He streaked from the cabin,
the lantern banging against his leg, and flung himself atop the
loyal jenny. He jerked her head around, gouged her with his
bare heels, and his nightshirt flapped around him as he raced
for help.

To Lizzie it seemed forever before assistance came. And,
when it arrived, it was through the person of Alton Wheeler,
not Rory Preston.

Alton's voice shook. He brushed flowing tears from his
eyes as he stared down at his boy, a heartbeat away from what
seemed certain death—if he hadn't departed earthly life
already.

Jem's handsome face was puffed and discolored, an inden-
tation on his head made Alton's stomach roll over. Alton felt
as if a part of him were dying.

A massive sob shook him. "Is my boy dead, Lizzie?"

Lizzie sniffled her answer, her voice cracking with more
tears. "Not yet, Pa, 'n' I'm praying that the Lord'll let him
live. Oh, we need him so!"

"Bad as he's hurt, Lizzie, it may be a blessin' if the Lord takes him. . . ."

"Don't say that! I want him to live!" Lizzie cried. "I want him to live, no matter what!"

"Mayhap the Lord'll let Jem live," Alton said softly. "But I'll not allow that mule precious life! His breaths are severely numbered. I'll kill him myself—like I wanted to do this very afternoon. Oh, in the name of God, why didn't I insist?" Alton cried brokenly. "Where's Jem's gun?"

"In—in the pasture. It's broken, Alton. The mule stomped it. The barrels are bent. The stock's busted."

"Where's the poleaxe? I'll cleave that he-devil from ear to ear."

"In the shed . . ."

Ordinarily, a mere man, even one as big as Alton Wheeler, couldn't stand a chance, pitted against a mad mule. Yet, Alton's grief was such that, like Lizzie's, it would enable him to do what otherwise could not even be done.

Alton didn't even halt for exact directions to locate the ax.

Lizzie heard the shed door bang and knew he'd found it. She fled to the door, hating to leave Jem but fearing Alton's safety more. He was impervious to her begging shrieks, deaf to her pleas. He stormed into the pasture.

Cries as from the very pits of hell resounded, echoing over the land.

Thuds.

Curses.

Screams.

Lizzie covered her ears and bawled, but still the bloodcurdling sounds refused to be drowned out.

When Lizzie feared that he would not return, Alton appeared, silent, his eyes sad, his clothes drenched with darkening blood. He looked at his clothes and the expression on his face seemed to signify that he'd sought restitution for his son.

"He's—?" Alton murmured, then his voice trailed off as he was incapable of posing the fearsome query.

Lizzie sighed. "Jem's still breathing," she whispered.

"Thank God, I've been prayin' for him," Alton groaned the words. "Although my own fury and violence has probably been an abomination to Him. The Doc's here," Alton said when he heard carriage wheels clattering near the gate in the front yard. "Miss Abby and Lester went to fetch the physician."

The doctor came in, frowned, checked Jem over, then left a green bottle of a brackish looking painkiller for Lizzie to attempt to administer. He advised her on how to treat the cuts and bruises.

When he left, stating that there'd be no payment accepted by him because there was really nothing he could do, Lizzie knew his diagnosis: *Imminent death!*

So soon a wife . . . sooner yet, a widow . . .

Lizzie held Jem's hand every moment when she was not busying herself to tend to his needs. It was as if Lizzie believed that she could transfuse Jem with her strength, her grittiness, yes, even her . . . mulish determination that he should live!

chapter
8

As DAYLIGHT seemed to tiptoe into the world, unwilling to rudely startle slumbering mankind, although Lizzie's spirit was more than willing to stay awake, her body was weak, and her puffy, red-rimmed eyelids drooped shut, allowing her precious moments of needed rest.

When the bantam rooster crowed from the henhouse, Lizzie startled awake.

Momentarily she was disoriented as if she'd been caught in the clutches of a bad dream, but then she recognized her reality and raised her face and shook sleep from her eyes.

Stiffly, reluctantly, she boosted herself from the chair she'd drawn close to where Jeremiah lay in their bed. She removed her cramped hand from her husband's limp grip.

Her breath caught, and for a moment despair pierced her heart. Jeremiah lay so still that she believed he'd died and gone on to his reward while she still slept, unable to keep vigil with him, just as the apostles had grown too sleepy to wait with the Lord on the night when He was betrayed.

"Oh, thank God!" she whispered in fervent relief when she detected the slow, steady rise and fall of Jem's chest. He was alive! And as morning dawned, so clear and perfect, she drew from it an omen of hope.

Crossing the cabin on stealthy feet, Lizzie opened the kitchen door a crack and peered outside. She was quiet in her movements so as not to arouse the children. She knew that they required their rest, but she also was aware that she needed to postpone the relentless, worried questioning that would begin when they awakened for the day and tried to assimilate what had happened during the night and align it with what the future would bring for the family.

The morning was nippy, and Lizzie snugged her wrapper around her more tightly. Her breath steamed out into the chilly air, and the rooster's crow seemed almost crystalline, floating on the thin, icy breeze.

Frost clung to dead grass and weeds, appearing feathery and delicate, as it was tinged a shell pink by the blazing blood red sun that was lifting above the eastern skyline.

Lizzie decided to haul in the day's supply of water. She shuffled into a pair of house slippers but didn't bother to reach for a coat or cloak. Her teeth chattered as she stepped outside and the wind pierced her faded robe.

She clanged the pump handle a dozen times before water gushed into her bucket. The sluice of water had no sooner ceased than she recognized the hoofbeats of a lone rider on the trail.

Lizzie glanced from her posture bent over the heavy wooden bucket. She flicked her tangled brown hair from her face, and fought down a wave of nausea brought on by sleeplessness and the gnawing fear that held her entrails in its tight grip.

She was curious as to what neighbor was up and about already. Then the traveler came into sight.

Rory!

In a fleeting instant she remembered what, in her haste and heartbreak the night before, she'd been too upset to dwell on,

116

and had conveniently pressed from mind. And that was the fact that she'd sent Lester riding after Rory, but he'd returned with Alton Wheeler, because he'd been unable to locate his uncle who lived alone at the farmstead recently inhabited by their late pa and ma.

"Rory, where have you been?" Lizzie asked when he drew near, dismounted, and tethered his horse to a fence post.

Her tone was colder than she liked but, she decided, no less cold than he deserved.

He gave her a flat stare, obviously displeased with his welcome.

"Out," his response was purposely vague. "I thought I'd stop by 'n' breakfast with you and your family before I go home. But what's it to you to be askin' where I've been in that haughty tone? I'm free, a man, and over twenty-one."

Lizzie's voice cracked. "I was concerned because I sent young Lester ridin' for you late last night—and you weren't home."

Rory seemed to bristle, like a youth about to receive a calling down.

"I'm old enough to be out 'n' around on my own without havin' to ask, or answer, to my big sister in the matter. It's hardly as if I need to venture out carryin' forth a note endorsed by my sister, bearing her permission for me to be gone from home and hearth."

"Rory!"

"Where I've been's my business, Lizzie, so whyn't you just tend to your own?" Angrily he unwrapped the reins. "And forget about me eating breakfast with you!"

Lizzie placed her hands on her hips and glared at him.

"You might call to mind that you ain't been invited!" she shot back. "And as for where the tarnation you've been, young man, maybe I'll sure as blue blazes make that my business, Rory Andrew Preston! You're not too big to whup, you know! I'm startin' to think you could use the thrashin' o' a lifetime! Might whip some sense into you."

Rory rocked back on his good leg, grinning.

"Yeah? Well, since you're so busy shootin' off your mouth, Lizzie, perhaps you'd like to tell me who's a-gonna do it? Pa's gone. So's Ma."

Lizzie gave him a stern stare.

"Then the honor falls to me! I—I will!" Lizzie declared vehemently. At the moment, weak and weary as she was, she didn't doubt for a moment that feeling as righteously riled as she was, she could've done it handily.

Rory laughed harder.

"You? 'N' who ya gonna get to help you? Jeremiah?"

At the mention of her husband's name, and with Rory's attitude that she, perhaps even helped by Jem, would be found wanting in the strength to deal with a defiant Rory, caused her to remember the accident.

Anger turned to anguish. Threats gave way to uncontrollable tears.

The sight unnerved Rory Preston. It seemed to finish the task of completely sobering him.

Apologetically, he reached for her even as he seemed not quite certain what he'd done to wring such reactions from her.

In her hurt and anger, Lizzie shook away his touch, hissing like a frightened, furious, undomesticated barn cat.

"Lizzie! What's wrong?" Rory asked. His lower lip trembled as his eyes grew huge with confusion. "I was only teasin' you, Lizzie. You should know that. I was just makin' a joke—"

"Well it ain't amusin'," she sniffled, turning her face away from him. "It's disgustin'. 'N' I'm in no mood for funnin'."

She gulped in a steadying breath, and halted on the rock beneath the side door, refusing Rory's offer to let him carry the heavy bucket for her.

"What's wrong, Lizzie? How come Lester rode for me last night when I was . . . out?"

"Jem's hurt. There was a bad accident here last night. My husband's layin' at death's door."

Rory's complexion drained pale, then colored with shame. He stood, frozen, seeming reluctant to consider himself welcome in Lizzie's cabin now without an express invitation from her, and she was in no hurry to bid him entrance.

He finally managed to speak. "That's why you sent for me?"

"Yes!" Lizzie shot back over her shoulder.

Then she gave an impatient nod of her head, the curt jerk being the most gracious invitation she could manage at the moment as she concluded that Rory could come in, or stay out, whichever suited him best.

"'N' while my husband was layin' near death, you were out—well, God knows what you were doing—and I don't want to hear so much as a jot and tittle of what travesties you were committin'. Mama and Papa must be spinnin' in their graves over your carryings on, Rory Preston!"

"What happened to Jeremiah?" Rory ignored her chastisement and tried to change the subject.

"Mules!" Lizzie said as if that one word said it all.

"That jack of Lemont Gartner's?" Rory gasped.

"None other."

"Hasn't that man done us enough damage already?" Rory exploded.

Lizzie bit her lip and heard her brother out. For her, the worst realization in hearing his blaming words, flung out fast and in fury, was that she knew the basic falsity of the seemingly logical rationale.

119

She recognized that it was unwarranted malice, undeserved blame-laying towards a neighbor whose heart was surely grieved over how his idle—even potentially generous—action had spawned only agony for a family in the neighborhood.

"The misfortune for Mama and for Jeremiah ain't really Lem's doing," Lizzie tried to correct Rory's personal view. "He's no doubt feeling as bad as us over Mama. Mayhap even a notch or two worse, 'cause he's so nettled by guilt. He doesn't know about Jeremiah yet, but I know his heart'll be sore with the news. He'll wish he'd given that dad-blasted mule the bullet betwixt the eyes he was talkin' about, 'stead of gifting him to my man."

Rory gave his sister a disgusted, disbelieving look.

"Go ahead, Lizzie," he said, his tone heavy with sarcasm, "be a Bible-thumping, mealy-mouthed, do-gooder, full of forgiveness and compassion, loving those who hate you, returning kindness to those who give you cruel treatment. You can forgive Lemont before he even has to ask for it—but I can't and I won't. I'll hold the old goat accountable until my dyin' day!"

"He's not an 'old goat'!" Lizzie raged.

She was about to add that Rory should mind his manners in regards to an elder, but suddenly she lacked the strength to exhort him as he deserved. Even so, a thousand words seemed to burn in her mind, pleading to exit from her mouth, but she kept her lips clamped shut. Then finally she allowed herself to make one comment, and it was not hers but His.

"'Judge not lest ye be judged,'" Lizzie wearily sighed a reminder, even though deep down in a dark corner of her heart she found herself hard-pressed not to acknowledge that her own human sentiments in some ways perfectly duplicated some of Rory's vitriolic feelings. "'N' I'll thank you kindly to keep a civil tongue in your house while sheltered beneath Jem's 'n' my roof. Mind what you're sayin' for my young'uns to overhear. . . ."

Quietly, efficiently but numb, Lizzie worked, saying nothing while Rory dogged in her footsteps, getting in the way, but she was already too piqued with him to dare criticize him further for fear that once started there'd be no stopping.

As for Rory's attitude, it seemed painfully evident on his pinched features that even though his big sister had given him what-for, he seemed to prefer being with her—what family still existed for him—than to depart and be alone to reckon with his fears and failings.

"Can I see him? Jem?" Rory finally asked.

Lizzie gave him a quick glance. "He won't know ya," Lizzie whispered permission, "but you're welcome to take a peek at him. 'N' if you're in the mind, and can bring yourself to do it truthful and sincere-like, with a humble and trusting heart, Rory, I'd appreciate you prayin' for my man. . . ."

Rory followed Lizzie to the bedside. He stood mute, stricken, as he stared down at a bruised, battered, bleeding Jeremiah.

He regarded Jem a long moment, seeming unable to remove his gaze from the discolored, oozing flesh that was his brother-in-law but bore little resemblance to the man who'd been hale, hearty, and handsome as recently as the afternoon before.

The room seemed to sway around Rory as he stared. He felt his face drain, and he knew that his complexion probably had become even pastier than his skin had seemed when the mirror above Lizzie's washbasin reflected his dishevelment at him minutes before and his eyes had appeared like two raisins dropped in clabbered milk.

He felt a cold sweat pop out in his armpits and prickle

down the hollow of his back. He wasn't sure that he wasn't going to get sick and dry-heave right there in front of his sister from the effect of the vision confronting him.

Rory felt his stomach start to roll over. It gave him the will to tear his eyes from Jeremiah's still form. But the look in Lizzie's eyes was almost as painful for him to see.

Before he could censor himself, Rory spoke.

"Pray for him to live, Lizzie?" he whispered in disbelief.

"Yes," she replied. "We'll pray together." Stunned, Rory curtly shook his head.

He took a step away from the bed.

"I'll not pray such a thing," he hissed. "Better he should be dead. Not that I'll trouble myself to plead for that outcome, either. Despite everyone's combined babblings to their so-called Lord and Savior, it seems that this God, whoever He is, or people think Him to be, does pretty much whatever He chooses. Mankind's lives are lived out like—like—like a sick joke!"

"Rory, you can't mean what you're saying!"

For an answer he cursed, then continued.

"Horrible wretches, evil men, *they* prosper and know good times, while the people fool enough to live in humility, serving others, doing what they think God would want, instead of what they'd actually like to do, get the short end of the stick. They suffer to the degree that the worldly have fun and flourish!"

Lizzie gasped, stricken. She knew the logic of Rory's accusatory words. Such philosophies had probably been leveled against those who tried to do good since the very foundations of time, those who failed to understand that there was a place with many mansions, where justice was met, and a righteous reward given, where all powers worked toward good.

Lizzie gasped, stricken. "How dare you? How dare you rail on like the most hardhearted of godless unbelievers? How dare you spite and spurn the One who knit you in our mama's womb? Where, in such a blessed, God-fearing household, Rory Preston, did you learn such offensive blaspheming ways?"

Before Lizzie could stop herself she smacked him hard across his stubbly cheek.

Rory didn't flinch. He didn't get angry. For a long, long moment he stared at Lizzie with hollow, hurt eyes. Then he tenderly massaged his cheek where the imprint of Lizzie's hand blazed crimson against his sickly pallor.

"He's beyond hope, Elizabeth," Rory pointed out in a strangely gentle tone, without malice, which at that point she'd almost have welcomed because it would have given her something to rail at.

"The Lord can heal him!" Lizzie insisted. "He raised the dead, made the lame walk, the blind see, the donkey talk—"

"It's a pity He didn't have the courtesy to protect Jem from the mule so He wouldn't find it necessary to heal him," Rory pointed out in a dry tone. "Mama used to talk on about protection in the Lord, Lizzie. And you know as well as I that our mama was a good woman." Rory swayed unsteadily. "But she had to have been addlepated to bank on Christian 'protection' in the face of all that's befallen our family 'n' loved ones! Some protection! Sue Ellen Wheeler—a horrible death when all she was tryin' to do was bring about more life to serve God. Harm—crushed by a log! Me—a gimp, hobbling around on one leg! 'N' Ma—beat to death by the power of a lifeless contraption. Now Jeremiah, brained by a damnable beast. All Christians! Oh, don't talk to *me* about protection, because I no longer believe it, and will preach to you the folly of your faith . . . for 'tis no longer mine!"

Lizzie's burgeoning fury wilted.

"For the love of God, don't say such things," she begged, feeling fear on her brother's behalf that he wasn't competent enough to experience on his own.

"I'll say what I want!"

Then, as if to spite her purposely, Rory raged on until Lizzie covered her ears against the onslaught. She thought of the children—no doubt cowering in the attic, thunderstruck—listening to her brother and their uncle, ranting and raging like a madman with ideas counter to anything she ever wanted her young'uns to hear and at cross-purposes to everything that the Good Book said.

"Get out!" Lizzie screamed the order when she could endure no more and something deep within her snapped. She became as unrestrainable in her own way as Rory was in his. "Talkin' like that—you're not welcome beneath my roof. The Lord said that He would part father from son, mother from daughter, brother from brother, and while I knew His words to be true, I never dreamed that such division would happen in our own family, Rory, and cause me the heartbreak you've just delivered to me in seeing Scripture come true and such general prophecies fulfilled. But I place Him before all others. And I won't betray Him by allowin' you entrance to my home so you can rail against Him like a heathen, perhaps by your example underminin' what I've been trying to teach my young. You're evil, Rory Preston! Do you hear me? Evil! Don't darken my doorstep with your presence and more of your diabolical tirades! You're no brother of mine. . . ."

Grinning crookedly, his words neatly chopped off by her own, Rory turned on his heel and stumped toward the door. Lizzie felt an urge to call him back, but she bit her tongue to prevent herself from making the overtures. She had no need to ever beg his forgiveness for what she'd said—because the things he'd uttered were nigh on unforgivable.

With a heavily laden heart, Lizzie turned back to her work, weeping without cease. She suspected that the children stayed on their pallets long after they'd been awakened, because they could not bear to confront her as she dealt with her grief and despair following the ugly confrontation that they couldn't help but to have overheard.

Eventually her loud, wracking wails ebbed to become almost silent sobbing as she moved through her day, crying. She cried for Jem. She cried for Pa. She cried for Ma. She cried for Rory.

But most of all, she wept for herself and for the failings that could now be attributed to her because of her failing to keep a tight rein on her mouth as Scripture suggested.

The minute Rory had stumped away, decimated by her furious barrage, Lizzie had felt an odd urge to call him back, to run after him, to make him accept her hug, and to produce one of his own.

She'd felt an almost overwhelming need to make some semblance of peace with him, angry as she remained, and with such good reason for her wrath. But she stifled the urge and almost chewed off her lower lip to prevent herself from speaking rashly again and making such overtures to her recalcitrant brother.

In failing to give in to the needling desire to ask forgiveness for hurting him, she even felt somewhat better.

Well, she'd not go crawling to him, she later decided. And she had no need to seek his forgiveness for what hurtful—but true—things she'd raged at him. It was time someone told him a thing or two. . . . If Pa Wheeler could've heard such carryings on, Lizzie wouldn't have been alone in her lecture, for it would've become the testimony of two men.

With a heavy heart, Lizzie prepared breakfast, then called her children down.

They were silent, almost excruciatingly obedient, as if they feared that the least infraction would loose the wild woman they'd overheard fly into action that morning.

Alton arrived in the forenoon, and with his encouragement, Lizzie took a break from her labors and walked to the woods to pick roots and herbs with which to create steeped potions, and to fashion healing poultices contained within muslin and cheesecloth to apply to Jeremiah's many wounds.

Alone in the timber, Lizzie grew serene, and she had time to think and bring order to her chaotic thoughts.

And with the clear thinking came more tears, tears she'd tried to hold in after the children had arisen. She cried until she felt there could be no more tears left. But still there were.

She didn't bother to try to hide her emotions from Alton when she returned.

"What's wrong, Lizzie-girl?" he asked gently after shooing the children outside. "It's more'n just Jeremiah, although I'll grant you that's enough to have us all weepin' as you are. But what is it? Maybe I can help, Lizzie. And if not, the least I can do is pray about the matter."

"That's what is the matter. Praying. Actually, it's Rory. Well—"

Suddenly she was awash as she tried to sort out confusing explanations to make sense of the situation for Alton. She drew a ragged breath as she prepared to describe the day's dawning.

"Rory was here today. And—" When she fell into pain-filled silence, her back to Alton, and was momentarily unable to continue on, the older man misunderstood.

"Oh? And will he be by this evenin' to help the boys with the chores?" Alton asked.

"I doubt it, Pa. No. He won't be back, 'cause—'cause . . . I ran him off. . . ."

Dropping heavily to a chair at the kitchen table, Lizzie accepted a cup of coffee from Alton and accepted his grip as he held her hand while she told her story.

Alton gaped at her when she finished.

"You what? Oh, dear Lord, Lizzie, you what?!"

"I told Rory to leave and never come back."

"Something he did or said must've really set you off."

"He done both, actually," she admitted, but it was said in a tired tone that took no delight or comfort in blame-laying. Then she produced added details she'd withheld from her first telling of the morning's events. "He was blaspheming and mocking God and making spiteful remarks about Scripture. It was more than I could endure. And . . . I was awful, Pa. Like a woman possessed." She sighed and smoothed her hair away from her face. "Rory was bad in his way . . . but I was every bit as unchristian in my own behavior."

"When Rory returns, go to him in peace, girl," Alton suggested. "You'll feel better. So will Rory. You know how it is. A kind word will turn away another's wrath, Miss Lizzie. So go to him. He'll be too proud to return to a place from where he's been banished. That means you'll have to extend the olive branch o' peace. Let him know you're willing to let bygones be bygones, and start fresh."

"I will, Pa," Lizzie promised. "I'll have Lester watch the young'uns and Jeremiah, and I'll walk over to the farm and see Rory tonight. Take along a hot meal for him to have. I know he's not livin' right spiritually nor physically. I guess instead of banishing him, I should be drawin' him to me 'n' mine."

"Give him time, Lizzie, 'n' give him room, but most of all, keep on givin' him your love no matter how he nettles you. It's painful to watch someone turn against the Lord out of disappointment, anger, 'n' grief. But many a good person has done it. I did it. Jeremiah did it. Now Rory's doing it, as have so many others before him."

"You're right, Pa Wheeler."

"Don't trouble yourself unduly, Lizzie. Just remember that the Good Book is full of stories of great men who wandered away from the ways of the Lord, only to find the direction leading back to Him in the most unlikely of places. Just trust that the Lord works all things toward good. So even out of what seems the most evil implications can come the culmination of righteousness if that's what the Lord ordains. I'll try to stop by and have a word with Rory in a day or two myself."

"Oh, thanks, Pa. That'd mean so much to him, I know. He always held you in the highest of regard."

"A feelin' returned. Deep down, Rory's a good boy, and one day he'll be a much admired man you'll be proud to claim as your kin. Right now I expect he's woefully lonesome 'n' confused, perhaps needin' a man to be a pa to him. I'll see what I can do to help fill the void. 'N' Miss Abby, she does like to mother folks while we're waitin' for her to be entertainin' the motherly condition 'n' get in the family way."

"I'd be ever so grateful if you would. And I'll make a point of asking Rory's forgiveness this very evenin'."

Lizzie was haggard from work and worry, but as she traveled to the Preston farm her heart felt light as she'd washed away the dark, dank emotions and felt revitalized and filled with a capacity for love and compassion.

Rory wasn't home when she arrived. She waited around, but Rory did not show up. Lizzie poked around, found the water trough dry, the feed manger empty, even the grain pans containing nothing but dusty residue from oats that had been ladled out the day before. Or perhaps even the day before *that*. Anger started to burn within her breast again.

Will Preston had treated his livestock as well as he'd attended to his family, and it stuck in Lizzie's craw that Rory could be so flip toward his family and be just as irresponsible to the dumb creatures who depended on him for feed and water.

She returned home for a while, then late at night as the household was asleep, she hurried to the Preston farm. There it became clear that Rory would not be returning before the dawn so she gave up and walked home again her heart as heavy as it had ever been laden before.

Rory didn't return the next day, nor did he come home that night.

Nor did he show up by the next evening.

Already Lizzie's sons were doing chores at the Preston farm without having to be reminded to tend to the livestock on both homesteads.

Lizzie vowed to make trips to the Preston property, regular as clockwork, until she caught Rory home. Somehow she would make him listen to her. Surely, her words combined with Alton's calm exhortations would reach him.

Lizzie made dozens of futile trips before she realized that Rory had not returned at all once he had departed. Chances were good that he had no intention of ever returning!

"He's gone," a stricken Lizzie told Alton the following day. "'N' l—looks l—like he's gone for good."

"Aw, now, Lizzie, he may just be hangin' out, havin' good times around Effingham, and he'll end up comin' home eventually, and a changed man for all o' his worldly experiences."

"I'm hopin' and prayin' for that. At any rate, I left a note on the table asking his forgiveness, so it'll be the first thing he sees. He ain't slipped in and slipped back out, 'cause the note hain't been disturbed."

"I've not seen hide nor hair o' him in days," Alton said. "Nor has anyone I've happened to take into my confidence, askin' 'em if they've caught sight of him around Effingham or Watson. He doesn't seem to be in the area."

"Oh, no," Lizzie whispered.

"Not that that's any indication he won't return," Alton assured. "He could've decided to take a holiday to St. Louis or even Chicago."

"Well, I got enough to think about regardin' Jeremiah," Lizzie finally decided, giving in to the sharpness spawned by growing antagonism when she understood that Rory cared too little to consider his family or even the family livestock, "without troublin' my thoughts and wastin' worry on my brother when obviously none of us warrant such consideration on his part!"

"I'll stop by the farm 'n' do chorin' when I return home to Miss Abby and the girls," Alton offered. "It'd spare your boys havin' to make a trip over to attend to it."

"We'd appreciate that, Pa," Lizzie acknowledged. "Mayhap Lester, Maylon, Thad, and I can move the livestock over to our place in a day or two so it won't be such a burden."

"Let us know your plans," Alton said, "'N' Miss Abby can watch Harmony and Jeremiah while the rest of us attend to drivin' the livestock to your pasture so they can run with your critters."

Lizzie's three boys did such a conscientious job of attending to morning and evening chores on the Preston acreage that it was easy for a haggard, worried, eternally busy Lizzie to postpone moving the livestock from her parents' farm to her own acreage.

She tried to blot out the many reasons she had to worry, and she redoubled her efforts to try to set the tone for her family's attitudes by her own outlook and behavior.

In some ways it was easy for Lizzie to remain happy, for her joy knew no bounds each consecutive day that her beloved lived on, and she knew that chances diminished that he'd take a turn for the worse and die before she could do a thing to prevent his slipping away from her.

She made a point of being optimistic and stressing the good things in life while putting from mind the unpleasant aspects, or if acknowledging them, giving them short shrift as she spoke to her children with great hope for the coming dawn.

But, Alton knew, as Lizzie had to admit to herself, her brother's plight was never far from her mind.

When the second week passed, Lizzie was able to mark improvement in Jeremiah. All of her labors were rewarded in that moment of discovery, and she realized that no amount of hard work and compassionate nursing was too much to offer up if it meant that her beloved could be kept safe and not be called from this world and taken from her.

As her worries for Jeremiah lessened, her concern for Rory became a heavier burden to her mind.

On the eve of the third week, she saw lights through the woods in the early evening darkness and her heart quickened with elation and then was overcome by a wave of relief.

Her prayers had been answered.

At long last, Rory had come home!

Admonishing Lester to tend his pa and keep the fires warm against the winter chill, Lizzie filled the lantern with coal oil, wrapped a freshly baked loaf of bread in brown paper, and snugged her heavy cape around her. She set out walking over the harsh ruts as quickly as she dared.

The wind reddened her cheeks and made her eyes sting from the cold, but she found the evening exhilarating, and her heart was filled with such hope. She vowed that she wouldn't say so much as an angry word to Rory. She'd be as welcoming and without judgment as the Prodigal Son's father had been.

It would feel so good to give him a hug, and to brush his cheek with a welcoming kiss, to assure him that she and her family were thankful he'd returned again, and that they were there, waiting for him to visit and be welcomed in their cabin to share a meal and an evening with them.

So strong were the visions she entertained that the spectacle that confronted her when she rounded a crook in the road and climbed the gentle rise, was the antithesis of what she expected, and she gasped in confused astonishment.

Lanterns glared around the entrance to the cabin. A man— a man about her own age, perhaps a few years older, and a gaggle of curly-haired girls—were boldly carting possessions from their rickety wagon into her mama's house!

They were laughing, and their happy words rang in the air. There was no mistaking their intent: They were moving in! Upset to the point of calm anger, Lizzie strode up the road as fast as her long skirts would allow.

"What do you think you're doing?" A barely civil Lizzie demanded to know, even though it had been painfully obvious to her.

"We're movin' in, ma'am," the man said, and slipped off his glove, extending a warm hand to her. "We're your new neighbors. The Mathews family."

Lizzie felt herself swoon. She caught herself by gripping the rude slats of the man's crude tumbledown wagon.

"I'm sorry, sir, but you're not free to squat here."

The man's smile stiffened.

"We ain't squattin', ma'am, I bought this place fair 'n' square from a young bloke in Effingham who needed a grubstake to go seek his fortune."

"You *what?*"

His explanation was worse than her imaginings. "I bought this farm from a young gentleman who offered it to me at a good price."

". . . It wasn't his to sell."

The man patted his breast. "I have the deed right here in my pocket, ma'am." He reached in, extracted it, but she shook her head, refusing to look at it, for she sensed he spoke the truth.

"It wasn't his to sell!" she repeated, dazed.

"He said it was," the man replied. "He told me that he was his ma 'n' pa's only son and that there was not even a sister for him to claim."

Patiently, the man—Brad Mathews, a widower with four daughters—reiterated the situation.

He'd seen the young fellow around Effingham. The unkempt fellow had returned to town, went to the livery to sell his aged sorrel mount and Brad had been there when the unshaven young man had offered up his farm for sale, too, in order to raise money to take him—and a woman—to California.

Lizzie quailed. "Go on. . . ."

"The others, they had their little homesteads already," Brad said. "But for me it was like a dream come true. I've had a spell of bad luck in my time—although I well know that the Good Lord doesn't promise us an easy time of it in this world—and with my Missus a-dyin', and me trying to raise up my four young ladies by myself, money's been tight, and times hard."

"Yes, I'm sure," Lizzie murmured.

"This younger feller described this place to me—and one of the blokes at the stable—he allowed as how he'd passed through this community, and, that such a farm existed. So, me 'n' that young feller—your brother, I'm sorry to learn—

made a deal. I gave him my money—almost my life's savings right on down to the very penny—'n' he deeded me the farm." He held out the paper for Lizzie's inspection.

"Indeed he did."

"Ma'am, I'm powerful sorry about this turn of events—but, I–I—*we* have to stay here. Me 'n' my girls, this was to be our home. We've got nowhere else to lay our heads."

Lizzie sniffled. "I know," she whimpered. "It ain't your fault. You dealt in good faith. But, oh my God, I don't know how much more I can take."

"Ma'am, I can tell this farm means a great deal to you. My heart's heavy upon learning what's transpired. But, I bought the land and it's deeded to me. However, if you want the land back, you can reimburse me the money and it's yours." He paused. "How you get it repaid you by your brother—well, that's 'tween you 'n' him. That's my offer, ma'am. Though me 'n' my girls got nowhere to go. And, frankly, I like the looks of what I see."

"Welcome to Salt Creek community, Mister Mathews," Lizzie said. "On behalf of the neighbors I present you a cordial greeting and tender the hope that you'll have a long, happy, prosperous life in these parts with us."

His smile widened when he realized the farm was his. "Thank you," he murmured. "Girls! Make acquaintance with our new neighbor—Miz Stone."

One by one they thanked Lizzie for her greeting and passed their names to her, offering wee curtsies as they did.

"You've a fine family, Mister Mathews," Lizzie commended. "I know you won't remain strangers here long. You'll find the neighbors helpful, generous, and good folk of fine faith."

"I thank you, Miz Stone," he said.

"Uh . . . about my brother. You said that he left town?"

"That he did. I saw him get on the train . . . uh . . . with a . . . traveling companion. . . . No doubt his . . . intended. By now he's long gone. I'm sorry."

"So am I," Lizzie said, dazed. "And I'm afraid it may be my regret for as long as I live."

"Tell your husband that I'll be by to make his acquaintance," Brad Mathews said in a chipper tone.

Lizzie didn't reply—couldn't!

Wracking sobs seemed only a breath away. She couldn't tell him about Jem. With him new in the neighborhood he'd find out soon enough.

"Oh . . . here," Lizzie changed the subject and shoved the brown paper wrapped package into Brad Mathews's hands. "Bread. I baked it today. It may even still be a bit warm from the oven. For your breakfast in the morrow, or your supper this very eve."

"Why, how neighborly," he exclaimed. "Much obliged."

"And down in the root cellar, on Mama's shelves, you'll find jams, preserves, 'n' lots of good things to eat. My mama'd be proud if you'd help yourselves, 'n' nourish your growin' girls from the fruits of her labors 'n' the efforts of her hands."

"I reckon I'll be acceptin' your generosity, Miz Stone. This is everything we own right here." He gave a limp gesture. "'Tain't took us but a trip or two to lug it all into the cabin. But then we was led to believe. . . ."

"Rory sold you the place lock, stock, 'n' barrel?"

"That he did, ma'am. But I had no idea of the true situation when he assured us that it was ours to claim."

"Then it is," Lizzie said. "I—I won't dispute. Although it gives me a heavy heart—I'll abide so that my brother can be a man of his word—'n' rest easy knowin' that Mama was at her happiest when providin' for the needs of those less fortunate." She paused. She gave the shy girls a sweet smile. "I believe Ma

135

would've loved making your acquaintance. She'd have tucked your girls under her wing 'n' taught 'em all she knowed."

"My girls miss a woman's influence. Perhaps there'll be some generous-hearted ladies in the neighborhood—"

"I must return to my husband. He needs me. Goodbye— 'n' God bless you in your new home." Quickly she walked away. And she wept all the way home. . . .

"Ma, what's wrong?" Lester asked when he met her on the trail.

"Rory. Rory!" she sobbed. "He's gone. 'N' he sold Ma's farm. New people are livin' there already. He sold it lock, stock, and barrel! Nothin' of Mama's is mine!"

"Sold everything? But it wasn't—"

"Yes, sold it all! Every stick of furniture, every chicken in the coop. No doubt sacrificing it for a song! So he can spend the money doing God knows what—and I couldn't bear to hear!"

Even so Lizzie's heart was heavy with a desire to see him just one more time so that she could tell Rory that come what may, he'd always be a brother to her.

"Oh Lord," she groaned and searched the heavens, "You know where he is. Guide Rory. Take care of him. 'N' please continue to watch out for him, as You always have, when he hasn't the good sense to bother to do it himself. 'N' if it pleases You, let me see him, face to face, once before I die. He's all the family I've got left, God, all that's left. And I do love him. . . ."

chapter
9

"I HAVEN'T MET Mister Mathews yet," Miss Abby admitted to Lizzie Stone two days after the older woman had discovered that the man and his daughters had moved into the cabin where she'd once resided with her parents. "But Alton has. And he says that Mister and his girls seem very, very nice. I'm looking forward to having the Mathews girls in the class-room."

"Actually, he's very personable," Lizzie said. "Even so, it hurts knowin' that Rory thought so little of Ma 'n' Pa's memory and, obviously, of me, that he sold the family farm—lock, stock, and barrel—to a perfect stranger without giving me so much as a word's notice of his intent, when in doin' so, denied me the chance to claim so much as one thing in the way of family heirlooms."

Miss Abby was sympathetic.

She took a sip of her tea. "Lizzie, from what Alton's said, I believe Mister Mathews would be a reasonable fellow. Don't you think that perhaps if you spoke to him about your family's possessions, that he'd relent, and you could—"

Lizzie stiffened at the very idea.

"I'll not beg a stranger for the things belongin' to my mother, nor the items created by her industrious hands!"

137

"Oh, Lizzie, it breaks my heart to see you take on so. I'm aware you're not happy with the circumstances, but please realize that Mister Mathews and his girls are as much victims of the painful circumstances as you are."

"I suppose that's true," Lizzie sighed agreement. "And I do wish 'em the very best, exactly as I expressed it to them the night when we made acquaintance while they were movin' in."

"We can imagine that they packed their belongings with great hope for the future," Miss Abby said. "I know what I felt upon knowing that I'd be moving to a new community, to be welcomed by the area's people. Surely the Mathews family had hoped for no less than to be unreservedly accepted into the Salt Creek community. And even though I think people have stepped forward to make them feel welcome, deep down there must be prickly areas of discomfort as they realize that what seemed their good fortune had been met only at your expense. So they must fear that instead of being wholeheartedly welcome that beneath the surface appearances there's a lingering stain of natural resentment no matter how kind your initial words of welcome to them were."

"But I don't feel that way at all!" Lizzie insisted.

And as she said the words, she realized that they weren't hollow protestations, but that her explanations represented the unvarnished truth.

She realized that just as her family took their day's tone from her, so might the entire community—that it was up to her to give them an example that would make Pa and Ma Preston proud.

No sooner had Miss Abby and her little girls departed for home than Lizzie withdrew sugar and flour cannisters, sent Thad to the henhouse to pilfer fresh eggs out from under the hens so she'd have enough for the recipe, and she set to baking a moist and delicious vanilla pound cake.

She'd just put the final swirl in the icing and laid the knife aside when the boys trooped in from doing chores.

"A cake!" they gasped.

"Run a finger through that frosting, Thad Samuel Childers, and you'll live to regret it!"

"Aw, Ma. . . ."

"There's a cake for our family on the sideboard," Lizzie said, "to enjoy after y'all have eaten a good supper."

"Then who's this one for?" Lester inquired.

"It's a welcome-to-the-neighborhood cake for the Mathews family down the road," Lizzie said.

The children looked at each other. Clearly, Lizzie realized, they hadn't been sure how to react to the new children in the neighborhood, because they hadn't figured out how their mother was responding to having her family farm sold out from under her.

"Mister Mathews has some growin' girls," Lizzie said, "but it takes a few years and some practical experience to be able to bake the kinds of cakes Granny and I always made. So I thought they might enjoy an extra special treat to help 'em enjoy their new home all that much more, 'specially during these early days as they're busy gettin' settled in."

"Can we go along, Mama?" they all began to ask.

Lizzie frowned. "Not tonight, darlings. Lester will drive me in the wagon. The rest of you can remain here with your pa. Someone's got to mind Jeremiah."

"Oh, yeah," came the solemn answer, and Lizzie knew that already, there were times when Jeremiah had become like a piece of furniture. Something immobile. Something taken for granted. Just *there*. Something—someone—requiring little conscious thought until moments like the present instant,

139

when his requirements caused sacrifice from the children, too, and they remembered the realities of the situation.

The night sky was velvet black, and the stars shimmered with cold brilliance as Lester guided the wagon over the ruts to the Mathews residence.

Brad Mathews met Lizzie and her son at the door. He seemed surprised—and a bit cautious—when he confronted the pair.

"Just a little something to further welcome you to the neighborhood, Mister Mathews. I figured you and your girls had been too busy workin' at gettin' settled in to have much more time than to fix necessary vittles. Your hours are probably too precious right now to waste on fussy-type cooking."

A relieved grin wreathed the surprised fellow's face.

"I do declare, Miz Stone, in all of my natural born days, I've never seen a cake so fine. It could win a prize at the county fair, I believe."

"That's what my first husband, Harm Childers, always told folks, 'n' that's Jeremiah Stone's sentiments, too. But I never did get over that way to enter. It's a real far piece, y'know, though last year had it not been so hot, Jeremiah would've followed through on his plan to see to it that my baked goods got into competition. Not that winnin' would've been important to me," she hastily explained. "Havin' my family and loved ones enjoyin' my fancies is commendation enough. But you know how menfolk are, braggin' about their wives' kitchen deeds."

"Yes," Brad Mathews said, and a distant expression came to his features, "I do recall making just such claims about my dear Emily's cooking."

At the sound of conversation near the front door, one of Brad Mathews's girls appeared and he gave her the cake. He invited Lizzie and Lester into the cabin that had once belonged to their kin but now seemed a different abode altogether as the Mathews family's possessions had imprinted it with their personalities.

Lizzie hadn't intended to stay to visit, but once she arrived, she realized that they had little choice but to do so or to risk being viewed as rude, the gift cake notwithstanding.

Seeming pleased at having honest-to-goodness callers, Brad and his girls outdid themselves to make Lizzie and her son feel welcome.

When Fanny Preston's mantel clock chimed the hour, Lizzie realized how late the evening was and how quickly it had passed.

"You'll have to wind the mantel clock regularly," Lizzie said. "Mama always wound it thirteen times. And every Friday. I kept it wound while . . . while my brother was away from the cabin. I don't know that it'd harm the old clock to be handled otherwise, but if you've a mind to follow Mama's routine with that ol' relic, now you know it. It was pro'bly so used to her touch that it'd appreciate any little familiarity."

Brad gave a nod, but Lizzie noticed that it seemed a bit uncertain, and she hoped that she hadn't overstepped her bounds by seeming to try to tell him what to do.

"I—I found the key the other evening," he said, "when I examined the clock."

"Mama believed in keeping it handy. When Rory and I were little, she had to keep it hid. But your girls are old enough so they won't risk ruinin' the clock by toyin' with it out of turn."

The girls tendered good-byes, and Lizzie offered a general invitation for them to come calling.

"Mayhap be that we'll see you at church services on Sunday," she said. "I try to get there regular, though it ain't as

141

easy now as it once seemed to be. . . . My husband ain't a well man these days."

After delivering the cake, she and Lester returned home. Lizzie anticipated that they'd eventually have contact with the Mathews family, but it occurred sooner than she had expected, for the next day Brad Mathews's lackluster horse drew the decrepit wagon that was once again piled high with the earthly belongings they had moved to the Preston farm.

But now it was heaped with Fanny and Will's household possessions.

"I reckon you'd be wantin' these things, Miz Stone," Brad murmured softly. "I saw the fresh-dug graves that ain't even had time to settle yet, 'n' I realized the deaths were recent. I'm terribly sorry. Alton Wheeler happened by this morning. He's been a friend to me, so I asked his advice. He offered an opinion on the things we can live without that he believes you'd cherish having in your possession again."

She noticed that the mantel clock was safely resting on the wagon seat.

"Why, that's right thoughtful of you," Lizzie said, smiling.

"Your husband, is he better today?" Mr. Mathews inquired.

Lizzie shook her head and smoothed a stray lock of hair into the sleek coronet at the back of her head.

"There's been no change, I'm afraid. It's been some weeks now. And I—I'm about to give up hope. Body 'n' soul are still together, he's not losin' ground, mind you, but he ain't makin' progress on his wits returnin' to him. I try to remain optimistic, for my sake, the young'uns, and for Jeremiah's, but I have my moments of feeling plumb fainthearted."

A shadow crossed the pleasant man's features.

"Oh, now, don't be doin' that, Miz Stone," he cautioned.

"It's hard not to," Lizzie admitted, "when Jeremiah lays still as death. Not movin' a'tall. Not openin' his eyes. Not speaking. 'N' it takin' so much time for me to coax broth and puddings into him so's to nourish him 'n' keep up his strength. . . ."

"It stands to reason he might be in a coma a while after the blows to the head that the mule gave him," Brad said gently. "Alton told me about it. And I'm no doctor, of course, but I've heard tell that some folks comes out of a coma perfectly all right. And after a rather extended spell, too, when folks thought they'd never come to again."

"I've been told as much," Lizzie said. "But frankly, I thought that people were simply trying to boost my spirits 'n' jolly me along so I wouldn't give up in despair. I worried that they were thinking it was hopeless but were too polite to say so."

Brad shook his head.

"Heavens, no, Miz Stone! Folks around here don't seem that they could be so cruel as to offer false hope. You just buck up and be brave. You've got to keep your hopes up. Otherwise it'd be nigh on unbearable. I know what it's like," Brad said in a soft voice. "My Emily . . . she died a lingerin' death."

"I'm so sorry," Lizzie murmured.

"Living through what I did, I've come to the conviction that it's harder by far watchin' a loved one slip away by inches 'n' degrees when there is no hope for recovery. At least if your man comes around again, he's got a healthy body. He's not wastin' away with a consuming disease."

"That's true."

"Anyway," Brad said, getting down to the business at hand. "We picked through your ma and pa's things to find items I felt you'd be in a notion to want. I'm not a good judge of what a gal would treasure, so I asked my young ladies for their input, and they helped some, then Alton passed judgment, too, and helped me load the goods. But if I failed to cart along something you'd especially like returned to you—consider it yours."

"You've really been so kind," Lizzie said. "I—I know you paid Rory for all the items. You don't have to."

"Don't have to, ma'am, but want to. I know how I'd like for me and my kinfolk to be treated if we found ourselves in such straits. I can unload the cartons and barrels where you specify if you've figured it out by now, Miz Stone."

"Just a moment and I'll fetch my wrap. Jeremiah and Harmony will be all right no longer than it'll take me to assist you."

Mr. Mathews backed his wagon to a side shed, and between the pair, the cargo was promptly unloaded and stowed in the shed for Lizzie to sift through items at her leisure, assigning items to their proper place in her household.

Brad Mathews lugged the mantel clock into Lizzie's cabin and set it on her kitchen table when they'd finished the task.

Lizzie removed her woolly scarf from her tresses.

"I can't thank you enough, Mister Mathews."

"Seein' the joy in your eyes at possessin' your mother's handiwork and household treasures is payment enough," he assured.

"As cold as the day, and as long as you've been out and about, loading, unloading, and journeying to our farm, won't you have a cup of tea? Or a cup of coffee? I've already got the kettle heating and there's leftover coffee from this mornin'."

Brad Mathews removed his hat, gloves, and coat. "If you're sure it's no imposition," he agreed.

"None whatsoever," Lizzie said. "If I might be so bold as to make the remark, quite frankly, I'll relish the company. With cold weather upon us, neighbors don't get out and about as handily as before. Visitin' your family last night was the first

I've been out in a spell. For me, news's been scarce. I'm hungry to hear what all of the neighbors have been up to."

"Well, that I can provide," Brad said in a jolly tone. "The folks have been right friendly in makin' it a point to stop by and welcome us to the community."

"Then do tell!" Lizzie gaily invited.

She checked on Harmony, who continued to nap. Then Lizzie crossed the cabin to the area that comprised Jeremiah's sickroom. Mr. Mathews trailed after her. He hesitated in the open doorway.

"This's my husband, Jem," she said softly, "Alton's son."

"Handsome fellow," he observed.

Lizzie gave him a quick smile. She touched Jem's brow and smoothed his hair from his forehead.

"I like to think so, but then I'm afraid that I'm rather partial."

"As a wife should be," Brad Mathews whispered. "As a father, I'm afraid I'm not without bias about my girls' beauty."

"They're most attractive," Lizzie assured. "Comely, and they seem sweet-mannered, too."

"In my judgment they are. A lot like my dear Emily was."

"I'm afraid that I was in such a state the evening when y'all moved in and last night, for that matter, that your girls' names have plumb slipped my memory."

On familiar territory, Brad Mathews seemed to draw greater confidence and became at ease,

"Linda's the oldest. Then comes Jayne, Patricia, and Rosalie."

"What pretty names," Lizzie said, "and worn by such handsome girls. They must be a wonderful consolation to you."

"That they are."

"No doubt tremendous help, too."

"Well . . . they try," he agreed, but in such a careful tone that Lizzie realized there had been problems within the household. "They do right well, actually, the best that they can. But bein' a man, there's so much I can't teach them . . . don't know how to teach them . . . or remain ignorant of what there's a need for the girls to even know."

"I know how that is," Lizzie commiserated. "'N' I'm woefully aware of how it'll grow worse for my boys if Jeremiah doesn't come out of this sick spell with his wits about him."

"I'll be pleased to help you out if there's anything me or my girls can do to ease your plight."

"So far Alton has seen to our needs," Lizzie said. "But I appreciate your kind offer."

"It's more than polite chit-chat, Miz Stone. It's a heartfelt suggestion. We want to be neighborly."

"I'll be grateful for what help and influence you can provide my sons, but I will more readily accept it if you'll allow me to aid your growin' girls. I know it can't be easy for them with no mama, nor a wise granny to fill in."

"Frankly, Miz Stone, I was kind of hankering for that offer. My girls, they're pining for a motherly woman's attention. It ain't my intent for them to make pests of themselves, but I would be most grateful if you'd warrant 'em a few minutes of your time, 'n' guide them in the ways of upstanding, refined womanhood, make them at home with the household arts."

"I'd be delighted to help guide your girls."

"They'll be willing protégées. My girls are still talking about that cake you baked and decorated. I'm afraid it was such a sweet treat we'd slickered off the platter by this mornin'!"

"Then we'll consider the arrangement good as accomplished," Lizzie promised.

He nodded. "I thank ya, Miz Stone. I'd best be headin' on home."

"If you're not in a big rush," Lizzie said, "you're welcome to stay 'n' warm your bones with a bowl of soup."

"It sounds good, but—"

Lizzie threw caution to the wind.

"But you're still welcome," she assured. "There ain't likely to be many folks out and about in such chilly weather. And, for that matter, it ain't exactly scandalous behavior to eat a bowl of soup with a neighbor. That seems the least I can do in thanks for your so kindly returning of Mama's things to me."

"And I do have a weakness for good soup."

Quickly Lizzie set the table, sliced dark bread, and placed butter churned the day before, in the center of the table, next to a pot of blackberry jam. Then she hefted the tureen to a cast-iron trivet.

Lizzie shoved the high chair up to the table, wiped a sleepy Harmony's face with a warm cloth, then folded the small child's hands together as Brad pronounced the table grace.

Lizzie ladled out the thick soup and then oversaw Harmony's childish efforts as she fed herself. Lizzie didn't have to ask twice to get Brad to accept a second serving of soup.

Quickly Lizzie ate her cooling soup, then she mashed vegetables strained from the broth and carried the warm gruel to the bedroom. Slowly, painstakingly, she fed Jeremiah as Brad rocked Harmony. A long time passed before Jem's bowl was empty.

As Lizzie entered the kitchen and Brad laid the sleeping Harmony on the horsehair sofa, Fanny Preston's mantel clock bonged.

"Great Scot! It's later than I had realized," Brad said, startled.

"How time's slipped away," Lizzie agreed.

Lizzie walked Brad to the door and waved as he drove his horse and wagon home. When the new neighbor was gone, Lizzie felt oddly alone as Harmony dozed and Jem lay still as death.

Two days later Brad Mathews returned with his young'uns. The girls remained in the house with Lizzie, and, quite naturally, Brad allowed Lizzie's boys to lead him outside. They were a long, long time returning. When they did, the boys' talk was full of the conversation shared with Brad Mathews and the interesting things he'd told them.

The household seemed subdued when they settled down for their evening meal after the Mathews family had departed.

"I really like Mister Mathews, Ma," Maylon said. "Do you?"

"Um. Yes. He seems a very nice fellow. Salt of the earth. He rather reminds me of Alton. Pa Wheeler. . . . Not in looks, mind you, but in temperament, and in shoulderin' responsibilities and doin' for others afore he tends to his own needs."

"He does," Maylon agreed.

Lizzie fell silent as suddenly she realized her impressions of her new neighbor were as confusing as her reactions to his presence in her old home and as her neighbor.

"The other day Mister Mathews said—," Thad started anew.

And as Lizzie scarcely listened on, the boys were discussing their new friend in the awed and admiring tone that had previously been reserved only for Alton, Will Preston, Jeremiah, and sometimes, during better times, their Uncle Rory.

Although she couldn't quite pinpoint exactly why, Lizzie felt a strange sensation, a feeling of unease in their discussion of the man and what she recognized as the quick development of devotion to him.

She was drawn up short when she felt almost as if they were betraying Jeremiah by helplessly liking and admiring Brad Mathews as they did. She felt needling guilt when she realized that in her life that had grown devoid of conversation and companionship, her thoughts, too had suddenly begun to fill with things Brad had said to her while Jeremiah was locked in a world of silence.

"Best do your studies, boys," she admonished, causing them to cease chattering. "I have to tend to your papa."

Soon the children readied for bed.

Lizzie delivered hugs and kisses, then she took time to read a chapter from her Bible.

"Let me hear your prayers," she said, and folded her hands expectantly, closing her eyes as she waited.

They began, Lester first, then Maylon, Thad, on down to Harmony, each one in turn mentioned their special thanks for blessings of the day and offered hope for the Lord's attention to a pressing problem they felt unequipped to handle without His strength and wisdom.

"Amen," Lizzie echoed.

They came to her for bedtime hugs and kisses.

"Good night, darlings! Sleep tight!"

Hastily Lizzie bathed and slipped on a crisp nightdress that was cold to her touch as she pulled it from her dresser drawer in the chilly bedroom. She seated herself on the edge of the tick. Her motions rocked the bed. She drew the comforters back and slid beneath their heavy warmth. Her bare calf brushed against Jem.

"Good night, Jeremiah," she whispered.

There was no answer.

"I love you. . . ." she added.

But, of course, there was no reciprocating response.

Not that Lizzie had expected one.

149

She considered the nights of togetherness and physical communion they'd once shared, and she felt suddenly hollow and dead inside. Weeping silently, so as not to arouse the children, Lizzie rolled over, threw her arms around Jem, and clung to him.

Hot tears dropped, one by one, to pool below her cheek as she listened to his heart pound with such a steady rhythm even as his body and mind remained so still it was as if his soul had departed already.

She thought about Rory's opinion that Jem would be better off dead. But Rory was wrong. Better that Jem was with her as he was than gone forever, leaving her totally without a hope—that one day he would wake up and be a husband to her again.

Lizzie raised up on her elbows and lightly kissed Jem's soft, unresponsive lips. A teardrop fell from her cheek to his. Then she hugged him close, even as her embrace was not returned.

"For ever and ever, my darlin'," she whispered, "that's how long I'll love ya 'n' be true to you. Until for ever and ever. . . ."

chapter
10

A WEEK PASSED. Thanksgiving bore upon them. Three days before the anticipated holiday, Alton arrived. He tethered Doc and Dan, then retrieved a burlap tote sack. He tromped through the light snow to Lizzie's door.

"Pa Wheeler!" she cried, delighted.

"I brought somethin' to you, Lizzie," he said, hefting his solid burden. "Turkeys. For the Thanksgivin' meal."

"How wonderful," Lizzie said. "But how did you—?"

"They're wild toms. I hope they won't be too tough."

"I'm sure they'll be delicious," Lizzie said. "I'm afraid I've been so busy I've scarcely had time to think about the comin' holiday, although that's about all the children talk about, as Miss Abby's been teachin' them about the tradition at school."

"Speakin' o' Miss Abby, Lizzie," Alton said. "That's part of the reason I'm here with two turkeys. I'm wonderin' if I could impose to ask a favor. . . ."

"Anything!" Lizzie assured.

"Could you fix a Thanksgivin' dinner for your own—'n' large enough to include my family, too?"

"Of course," Lizzie assured. "In fact, already I'd been toyin' with the idea and was waitin' for my chance to ask. Is something wrong, Alton? Is Miss Abby all right?"

"She's feelin' a bit faint-headed 'n' weepy," he admitted. "She's thinking mayhap she's in the family way. . . ."

"How wonderful!" Lizzie cried.

"We've been married quite a spell, 'n' Miss Abby's been hankerin' for a young'un, and, indeed, I hold tender to that notion myself. But Miss Abby, she gets tuckered out teachin' the young'uns, 'n' I thought maybe an invite to break bread at your table would set her mind at ease and give her the rest she's going to need."

"It will," Lizzie assured. "'Twill be a meal fit for a king and plenty of it." She paused reflectively, frowning.

"Something wrong?" Alton inquired.

"No, I just found myself wantin' to spread the joy. My thoughts wandered to that nice Mister Mathews and his gracious girls. I wonder if they'd care to join us for the day—"

"I'd allow as to how they'd probably be delighted. It's a time for sharing. With Brad 'n' his young'uns new to these parts, they'd probably treasure the idea more'n most."

"Then I'll ask them. Unless you'd care to do the honor on your way home?"

"I'll be glad to, Lizzie. In spite of all that's happened, Lizzie, y'know, we've truly got a lot to be thankful for."

"I know," she said. "It's just that sometimes it's easier to be more grateful than at others."

"That's true enough, Lizzie-girl," Alton softly agreed. "But maybe knowing the sourness of disappointment and unhappiness, by contrast, makes the sweetness that comes into our life seem even more special to experience and relish."

Lizzie refreshed Alton's coffee cup with steaming brew from the granite pot on the wood range, then poured another mug for herself. Wearily she seated herself across the table from him, smoothing her skirt that had grown damp from kneeling beside the copper boiler of hot sudsy water, grinding dirty clothing on the washboard.

"Speaking of things to be thankful for, Alton," she said. "I think there's been some improvement in Jem."

Alton's face took on new life. "You don't say!"

The first time Lizzie had thought that Jem had shifted position, she'd told herself that she'd moved his body herself to prevent the formation of bedsores and that she'd simply been so absentminded that she'd forgotten to complete the task.

But as she dared to hope and then began to watch for signs of change, they seemed to be withheld from her. After she'd at last concluded that the supposed movement had been her imagination, and she'd relinquished hope, Jem moved again.

"He's thrashin' around a bit these days," she said, "'n' while it ain't much, it's a marked improvement over how he's laid still as a boulder for so long."

"That's good news, gal!" Alton said, elated. "Maybe there'll be more improvements."

"I'm prayin' so."

"We all are," Alton assured.

The day before Thanksgiving was a rainy one, but as the temperature dropped, it promised that the precipitation could change to become snow by the new dawn.

Lizzie kept the wood range fired. She baked the turkeys, attending to them with a careful eye. She basted them time and again, letting the flames in the stove die lower so the birds would roast slowly.

When she stepped from the kitchen, she heard Harmony giggle. Then her daughter laughed again.

"Harmony Childers!" Lizzie cried. "Don't be teasin' and pesterin' your pa, honey."

"But he's funny, Ma! Jus starin' at me 'n' won't blink. . . ."

"Starin'? Your pa's eyes're open?"

Jem's eyes were open. As if that wasn't enough to bring Lizzie hope unbounded, before her very eyes he moved his leg beneath the covers.

"Oh, Jem!" Lizzie cried. She sat on the edge of the tick and flung her arms around him. "You're goin' to get well, Jeremiah. I just know it! You're goin' to walk 'n' talk again! You must . . . you have to . . . I need you so!"

The next morning Lizzie was up before daybreak. She roused the children and bid them to help. They were well-prepared for their guests before company began to arrive.

"We've got a heap to be thankful for," Lizzie announced. "Jem's showin' marked improvement." She detailed what had occurred.

"Even though it's movement we take for granted in ourselves," Miss Abby said, "the longest journey starts with one small step. Surely Jeremiah's on the road to recovery!"

"'N' how are *you* feelin', Miss Abby? Alton confided in me."

Miss Abby smiled weakly. "Fair to middling. I'm hoping that this time the wish will become our dream and not result in more disappointment for us."

"Brad 'n' his girls are here," Alton said, interrupting the women's conversation when he stuck his head in the kitchen.

"Welcome them if you would, Pa."

Steam flew as Lizzie took lids off kettles and began to fill bowls, platters, and tureens.

"Dinner's on!" she sang out. "Come gather 'round!"

They bowed their heads as Alton prayed.

"This's the best Thanksgivin' meal I've had in years," Brad said after Lizzie served pumpkin pie. "Not that my Linda hasn't done a fine job in the past," he added graciously, and smiled at his tousle-haired daughter.

Lizzie, Miss Abby, and the older girls cleaned up the kitchen. Alton and Brad discussed farming. Eventually the guests began talking about departing so they could arrive home in time to do choring in the fading daylight.

Lester, Maylon, and Thad did their own chores after the visitors had driven away.

Lizzie set supper on the table for her children, then took her own plate into the sickroom so that she could enjoy her meal with Jem so they could eat together on Thanksgiving.

His eyes seemed clearer, his gaze less dazed, and a time or two Lizzie thought he actually seemed to know that she was talking to him, although he made no move to answer.

Her own plate was clean, and Jem's bowl scraped empty before she departed the bedroom. His eyes drifted shut in sleep. She'd seen him doze that way so many, many times before the accident. Her heart overflowed with love as she regarded him, looking so dear and gentle. Where there was life, there was hope. Always hope. Hope for the morrow and what the Lord would provide to enrich their lives and rejuvenate their spirits.

"We've so much to be thankful for this year, Jeremiah," she whispered. "'N' next year when you're well again—we'll have even more over which to be give thanks. . . ."

One icy December morning as Harmony played with a tin of wooden spools, a mixing bowl, and a long-handled spoon, Lizzie worked with shears, wire, clean straw, and dull red buckbrush berries, to fashion a wreath for her parent's graves.

Brad had invited Lizzie to visit the burial sites any time she desired, but she'd been so busy that she hadn't found the time.

155

Now, as Christmas neared, Lizzie labored to create colorful wreaths to mark their final resting place.

She'd have it all done, she decided, so that some day when the sun was shining and the ground was dry and the weather fitting, she'd make a quick journey down the trail to the graves at the Mathews's farm.

The following Monday was a beautiful day, and Lizzie found herself straying to the window time and again. It was more like Indian summer than approaching winter, and Lizzie itched to escape the confines of the snug, neat cabin.

Harmony, too, was fidgety, seeming to want something to do, but expressed dissatisfaction over any suggestion Lizzie made. Lizzie realized that the little girl was suffering the same odd cabin fever that she herself seemed to be experiencing.

"I wish we could take a walk or something," Lizzie sighed when Harmony grew even more fidgety. But they couldn't do that, for Jem needed her. *Or did he?* she wondered.

Actually, she realized, Jeremiah would be safe the short while it would take to make the brisk walk to the gravesites. He wouldn't even know she'd been away. It wasn't as if she was going to selfishly while away the afternoon in idleness. And it would fulfill her plans to go to her ma and pa's graves and make them as pretty as possible in anticipation of the Advent season.

Lizzie bundled Harmony into her coat and tugged on her boots, latching the closures. The little girl insisted on helping carry a straw wreath woven with buckbrush and holly, and Lizzie gave it to her, watching carefully as she struggled beneath the unwieldy burden.

"Let Mama carry the wreaths now, Harmony. We're almost there," she said when the Mathews cabin came into view.

Lizzie realized that following the fall rains, surely the newly mounded graves would have already begun to level beneath

156

the force of the pounding downpours, relentless wind, and subtle heaving and straining of the ground as it thawed, then froze. She made a mental note that the boys could spend a Saturday morning retrieving dirt to level the earth if necessary.

But instead of finding the graves barren and ill-kempt, Lizzie was confronted by two gleaming whitewashed crosses bearing her mother's name and dates of birth and death, as well as one for her pa.

Buckbrush, bittersweet, and prickly holly from Fanny's prized bush in the yard were stuffed in an amber mason jar and were secured in place beneath each dazzling white cross.

Lizzie neatly positioned her wreaths, then stepped back to admire the effect.

"Like it?" Brad asked softly from right behind her, so close that a startled Lizzie shied against him.

"Y—yes. Very much so. How thoughtful of you to construct such lovely markers."

"I asked Alton for the dates so they could be as nice as I could make them and as personal."

"It was very kind of you. I've been so busy I've scarcely had time to do anything but tend Jeremiah's needs. Ma 'n' Pa's graves went undone. . . ."

"I found satisfaction in tending to it, Miss Lizzie."

"That's what Papa always said about keeping the best burial box he could construct on hand in the barn loft. A tradition my Jeremiah took upon himself with Pa's passin'. You'd have liked Pa. He was one to see to others' needs every bit as much as Ma did. They both were always looking out for those less fortunate."

"I'm afraid I'm not as selfless in my actions," Brad said, as if to temper Lizzie's admiration of his grave-tending duties.

"For 'tis my hope that some kind stranger will be moved to tend my Emily's grave . . . since I'm not there to see to it."

"I'm sure the Lord will touch someone's heart. He's so careful in seeing to our needs before we even reckon the need."

"Can I tempt you with a cup of coffee to warm you for your return home?"

"That would be nice. But I should go. Jem's by himself."

"Coffee'll only take a few minutes," he said. "You owe yourself a dram of rest, Miss Lizzie."

Brad brought them coffee and filled a small tumbler with apple cider from the cellar for Harmony.

"I reckon I'm sort of runnin' on at the mouth, Miss Lizzie," Brad excused. "The memories—they tend to overtake me more some times than others—'n' today so happens to be the anniversary of my Emily's death. Five years. Five long . . . long . . . lonely . . . years."

The big man's gentle eyes filled with the sheen of unshed tears.

Further words sank away. Lizzie didn't know what to say in the face of his enduring grief.

When Brad spoke again, it was to change the topic.

They made easy conversation until Lizzie glanced at the watch that was a brooch, a quality jewelry ornament that had belonged to her ma and her ma's mother and had been presented to her on her wedding day, as she would bestow it on Harmony when she took a husband.

"I must be goin'. I've stayed much longer than I'd intended."

Brad nodded. "And 'tis my fault you have, Miss Lizzie, because in your kindness you've served a solid listener."

"Listenin', 'n' carin' . . . that's what friends are for, ain't it?"

"In my book it is," Brad replied. "And, in my self-centeredness I forgot to inquire: How is Jeremiah today?"

Lizzie sketched in vague improvements as she thought she had detected them.

"We must pray—and be patient."

Lizzie gave a weak and wistful chuckle.

"You sound like my Jeremiah," she said. "He was always exhorting me to be patient. And, I am, I reckon. At least a heap more so than I used to be."

"It's something that's easier learned the older we get," Brad said.

Lizzie consulted her timepiece again. "I must really be going now. Harmony? Ready to go home, darlin'?"

"It's my fault you're late in leavin'. Allow me to see you and your little one to your cabin. I know you're a busy woman."

"That's thoughtful, Brad," Lizzie accepted.

Her tongue struck dumb, Lizzie followed Brad to the battered wagon. He boosted Harmony, then offered Lizzie a hand up into the wagon but ended up lifting her as he had lifted her small child.

When his large hands encircled Lizzie's waist she felt almost overcome with strange, unidentifiable emotions. She sensed, too, from the prickly, stretching silence that seemed to twang between them with its vibrant stillness that Brad was as poignantly aware of the unusual but hauntingly familiar tensions as she.

He placed Harmony securely between them on the seat, and she was soon lulled to sleep.

Brad offered to lug the sleeping child into the cabin. Lizzie crossed the cabin to check on Jem. For a moment she thought her eyes had deceived her. Then, she realized they had not and her heart knew no bounds in her joy.

Jem had edged up—almost sitting—propped against the

159

pillows. He was in a position fresh from the one in which she'd left him!

"Jem!" Lizzie cried.

His head did not turn. But at the sound of her shrill, elated cry, his eyes jerked to seek her location. He stared vacantly as if he searched his mind for memories but found them absent.

At Lizzie's cry, Brad came into the room, and she gabbled about the change, gesturing as she tried to explain.

Brad nodded. "He's gainin' strength, Miss Lizzie. Iffen he stays in bed all o' the time—his muscles, they'll fall to disuse 'n' fail him. Alton and I have been talkin' about this—Jem needs to be exercised, though, you've so much to attend to already. With Jem conscious, Miss Lizzie, 'n' tryin' to move about, who knows how fast he'll progress if we work with him regularly? Why, there's no tellin' how soon he'll be up 'n' about and leavin' this sickroom if Al 'n' I can hoist him up and get him ambulatin' again."

"Yes!" Lizzie clasped her hands together and clung to the radiant dream. "Oh, yes!"

"And maybe soon your man will even be rememberin' things in full."

"Oh, how I hope so. . . ."

"He'll likely be sort of like raisin' a wee child, Miss Lizzie, and you may have to teach him things he's one way or t'other forgot he knew."

"You're right, but I'll manage to do whatever it takes," she vowed.

"Alton and I will help."

"I'll be ever so grateful to the both of you for whatever assistance you can give in helping Jeremiah to recover."

"Glad to help, Miss Lizzie, knowin' that it'll make you happy and sustain your hope."

Brad checked his timepiece, then abruptly turned to depart.

"I'll drive the wagon to the school to fetch my young ladies, since I have the horse hitched," he said. "And by your leave, I'll drop in 'n' announce the glad news to Alton about his boy, 'n' seek his counsel as we plan for Jem's welfare."

Seeming to sense that Lizzie wanted to be alone with her joyful thoughts and optimistic hopes for the future, Brad excused himself and hastily departed.

Harmony continued to sleep as Lizzie tucked a cuddly comforter up around her cherubic face, smoothing her golden curls on the down pillow.

Bustling into the kitchen, Lizzie fired up the stove and then flung open the pantry door, scrutinizing her shelves of canned goods as she knotted a hand on her hip. She scanned the preserved foodstuffs and tried to figure out what she could quickly put together to create a celebratory dish for their evening meal.

She'd just gotten the menu plans well underway when there was a banging on her kitchen door. Humming to herself as she had been, she hadn't heard anyone approach on the trail.

Lizzie's cheerful attitude changed to sudden alarm as the banging on her kitchen door continued and sent the cabin to shaking from the force.

She crossed to the door. "Yes?" she answered, then looked down to see the small man standing on her stoop. "Well, hello!" She warmly greeted him when she peered beyond him and recognized the peddler's wagon.

Her heart ached at the sight.

"I know it's chilly, Missus, as evenin' is setting in," the peddler said. "But I was wonderin' if you'd like to step out to examine my wares? I have some fine notions and geegaws perfect to brighten a wee one's eyes on Christmas morn."

"Oh dear . . . ," Lizzie lamented.

She looked at the peddler's boxes and the enclosed black

wagon with red and gilt lettering, drawn through the countryside by a sleek, young horse.

Lizzie thought of the dwindling sums of money in the worn leather clasp purse she kept hidden away in a bureau drawer.

"There are some things I need."

"Then step right out, Missus, and look your fill! Would it be that the good man is home? I have some fine files, tools, 'n' such plunder as would appeal to a bloke."

Lizzie chewed her lip and shook her head. Then she forced a light but firm smile.

"I'm sorry, sir. Not today," she dismissed, not wanting to offer grim explanations. "Perhaps when you return again."

Lizzie drew on a wrap and followed him to his wagon. There, ever mindful of her finances, she made her pitiful selections, allowing herself to purchase only things that were dire necessity. She accepted the items and tendered the peddler coins.

"Will that be all, ma'am? Christmas is around the corner. While weather's been fit of late—mightn't it not make for an unhappy day if you're prevented a journey to town to partake of toys and geegaws there? Best be buyin' for the young'uns while you've the chance, I respectfully suggest, and as you can see my prices are competitive with the merchants in their fine stores in town." The peddler stopped with his sales pitch, perhaps fearing, correctly, that to continue on with persistent speech could be fatal to a successful transaction and appear to oversell the products.

Lizzie's will teetered back and forth. Firmly she forced herself to turn away from the temptation to look again.

"I'd like to, sir, but we can't spare the coin. We . . . we've had tragic times to face. Do, please, return to us come spring, and by all means, again this time o' year."

The peddler accepted her verdict.

"I understand," he said. "And how many young'uns might be in this household?"

"Four. Three sons and a daughter."

The peddler reached into a jar and with a flourish withdrew his hand. "A candy stick for each!" he said.

"I thank you with all of my heart, sir."

The peddler drove away, and with slow steps Lizzie re-entered the house and tucked the candy sticks away in her cedar chest so they'd be there come Christmas morn.

Her happiness vanished momentarily as she considered the barrenness of her cedar chest, although her children never lacked from the fullness of her heart and would never treasure idle trinkets above her love.

Even so, Lizzie felt bleak about the fact that she had no gifts for them. At least, through the generosity of the peddler, now there were candy sticks to present her young.

"Was the peddler here today?" Lester asked, when he came flying in the door after school let out for the day.

"Ummmhmmmm," Lizzie said.

"Oh, shucks!" he said. "We were hoping that he hadn't been to our farm yet so we'd get to take a peek into his wagon. Some of the boys said that he was at their homes yesterday, making the rounds in the community."

"He's been here and gone, son."

"I'm sure sorry we missed him. . . ."

"Maybe next time," Lizzie comforted.

That night Lizzie reflected on the day, on Brad's words, on the peddler's visit, and on Christmas Day not very far away.

"I wonder if Miss Abby, Alton, 'n' the girls would be our guests for Christmas?" Lizzie idly commented over supper. "And how is Miss Abby, Lester? My how time's passed since I got to chat with her. We didn't get much of a chance to discuss anything on Thanksgiving, it was such a houseful with us, the Wheelers, and the Mathews family. And lately Alton hasn't thought to mention how Miss Abby's doin'. . . ."

"Don't rightly know how she is, Ma," the boy replied. "But one of the girls whispered that she caught Miss Abby in the coatroom cryin' the day before yesterday."

"Crying?" Lizzie echoed, and felt a prickle of alarm.

"That's what she said. And her eyes did seem kind of red today, too, like she's got a cold, only she's not coughin'."

"Does she appear ill?"

He shrugged. "Not really. Mayhap a bit mopey."

"I hope it's nothing serious. I'll have to inquire of Alton and be sure to invite them to share Christmas with us. That could give Miss Abby a bit more ease."

"Can the Mathews family come, too?" Thad asked.

"If they'd like to. And if they don't have other plans."

Apparently they didn't, for when the Mathews family happened by, Lizzie's children issued an invitation before she could tender her own, but she backed up their words by underscoring her own intention along that order and they quickly confirmed that they'd be Lizzie's family's Christmas dinner guests.

Later on, when Alton came by to walk with Jeremiah, Lizzie invited them to Christmas dinner, too.

"That's an answer to prayer. Miss Abby's not feelin' too pert. I'd worried about her facin' the strain of fussin' more'n usual over a holiday meal."

"I know how that is," Lizzie said. "When the sight and smell of food makes you feel as if you'll never want to eat again—and at a time when you're eatin' for two."

Horrible silence swept between them.

Alton sighed. "I may as well give you the news. There's no

wee one on the way for us. That's why Miss Abby's been melancholy of late."

"Oh, Pa Wheeler. I'm so sorry. Miss Abby must be plumb devastated."

"She is. She's a-pinin' like I ain't seen her mope before."

"Then it will be good for her to come here for Christmas," Lizzie said. "It might take her mind off things for at least a little while. Mister Mathews 'n' his girls will be here, too."

"The more the merrier," Alton said, but his tone seemed totally without joy.

Christmas Eve day, Lizzie scurried around the cabin, straightening, shining, cleaning. Brad had promised to come by to walk with Jem. When Lizzie heard horsehooves in the yard, she didn't glance up.

"Halloo!" An unfamiliar voice cried a heartbeat before there was a pummeling on the door.

Lizzie crossed to the threshold, flung the door open, squinted out, and for a moment didn't recognize the squat man who stood before her. It was Lemont Gartner!

He dropped a burlap sack of goods at her feet. "For you 'n' your young'uns," he said in a gruff whisper. "With my best regards."

Then, before Lizzie could speak, Lemont strode to his wagon and flicked the horse with his quirt, and the beast hastily bore him home.

Stunned, Lizzie stared at the bulging totesack. Only the chill wind finally stung her into action. She stooped, spirited the bag into the pantry, then she opened it up.

Tears brimmed to her eyes when she saw the gifts. Piled around her were myriad items any child would relish calling his own. There were colorful toys that would pique the joy for any young'un. Thoughtful gifts for her. Even a present obviously intended for Jeremiah's use.

By the time she'd emptied the sack, it seemed that everything she'd seen in the peddler's well-arrayed wagon lay scattered around her feet.

Great, gulping sobs, purging in their intensity, washed any remaining trace of hardness from her heart, and made Lizzie feel cleaned with joy and the special love found in understanding the true meaning of Christmas.

Poor Lemont! A lonely old bachelor with no family to call his own, no one to turn to that he might be comforted in his guilt and grief. Lizzie realized the sad plight of her family had never been far from Lem's troubled thoughts and prayers.

Unable to know exactly what to do—and very likely uncertain how a gesture would be received if he tried—for months he'd done nothing. But during the joyous Christmas season, trying to make up for the sorrow even as he knew there was no way, he'd spent his money on a needy family, contenting himself that their lot was a little easier, a little happier, for his effort.

Lizzie envisioned Lem the next day—on Christmas morn—with no family to visit him, and no close friends where he might go to idle away the special day in fellowship with others. What would he have to eat? Would he bother preparing a special meal?

It was at that moment that the idea formed in her mind. They would have a special guest. Lemont Gartner would be a visitor in her home, a welcome diner at her table. She would have to ask Lemont herself, Lizzie realized, as no other messenger could deliver the invitation with the same conviction as she.

Lizzie felt regret that in the weeks and months since Jeremiah's accident, she'd been so busy with her own concerns that except for taking Rory to task over his blame-laying, she'd had precious few minutes to spare to think of Lem's plight.

She'd been too overwhelmed by her own circumstances to have the time or energy to put herself into his place and imagine things as seen from Lemont Gartner's personal frame of reference.

Truly, she hadn't really blamed him for their misfortune except in a human, failing little corner of her heart.

Grievous mistakes are sometimes made by rash action. But Lizzie realized that some mistakes, every bit as hurtful, are created by omission, as when she'd thoughtlessly failed to do what she so easily could've done.

Why hadn't she considered Lemont at Thanksgiving? Had she but invited him to break bread with them that day, she could've let him know that he was still considered a friend and neighbor.

No doubt he had condemned himself time and again for giving Jeremiah that mule. And very probably he had assumed that they found him convicted, too, and he had convinced himself that they wanted no part of him.

How little it would've taken, she knew, to have spared the elderly man agonized nights alone when he'd have probably given anything if he could've turned back the hands of time and done things just a little bit differently if only it would've resulted in Jeremiah's being safe and sound—healthy as he was when the maverick mule had resided in Lem Gartner's pasture.

Lizzie knew that what was meant to be was meant to be and that the Lord God did not make mistakes. He was sovereign. Had things worked out differently, it would've been because that suited the Lord's will as what confronted them would work toward eventual good.

Well, she would postpone no longer what she should've attended to weeks ago. She would take care of the matter just as soon as she could make herself presentable after cleaning up from providing her brood their supper.

Later, with Lester placed in charge of the household, Lizzie walked to Lemont's farm.

"Yoo-hoo! Lemont, are you home?" she hailed him as she drew near his farmstead.

At the sound, he crossed his cabin and peered out the side window, startled.

For a moment he looked fearful—as if he expected Lizzie to sharply order him to travel to her farm and return and take back what were unwanted gifts from him.

"Can I come in and speak with you for a moment, neighbor?" she asked.

"Sure," he said, a bit hesitant. Then, seeing Lizzie's warm smile, he tendered one of his own. "Come on in and make yourself at home. Step close to the fire. Can I fetch you a cup of coffee? A cup of tea?"

"Nothing, thanks," Lizzie said. "I can't stay long. I left the young'uns in Lester's care. He's turning into quite a fine boy. I'm proud of him."

"And you've a right to be. What can I do for you, Miss Lizzie?" Lemont inquired.

"You can honor us with your presence at our dinner table tomorrow noon when we celebrate Christmas with some folks from the neighborhood. And you can accept my apologies that I didn't think far enough afield to remember to invite you to dine with us on Thanksgiving when it was the same group. You're welcome to come, and we're hopin' you'll accept."

"Are you sure?" he asked.

She nodded and underscored the gesture with a smile.

"Never more positive about anything in my life. But now I'd best be gettin' home. It's a long walk."

"No it ain't," Lem said in a gruffly tender voice. "'Cause I'm goin' to drive you, Miz Stone."

Christmas was a memorable day.

At dawn the children arose, scampering with exuberance as they discovered the gifts displayed beneath the small cedar tree Alton had harvested and hidden away in the shed the afternoon before, for Lizzie to trim with strings of popcorn she'd made.

It was plainly evident which gifts were for each child—and those for Lizzie—carefully selected by old Mister Gartner. Thoughtful as Lemont was, there was even a gift for Jeremiah—a woolly neck scarf that would help keep him warm in his walks with Brad and Alton.

It was a happy day for Lizzie. She was tiring when, by late afternoon, the guests departed.

"For you, Miss Lizzie," Brad said and pressed a small item into her hand. "I'm beggin' of you don't be offended."

She closed her grip around the small, hard glass. Only after he'd driven off did she dare look.

Lemon Verbena cologne!

She would wear it—and enjoy the springtime of her thoughts while living out the long summer years of her life.

chapter
11

ALTON AND BRAD taught Jeremiah how to walk steadily again, how to control his arms, how to master his legs.

Lizzie instructed him in how to use a fork but didn't trust him with a knife of his own. She retaught Jem in what simple manners he would be expected to know and patiently worked to teach him basic facts of life in their day-to-day world.

"Jeremiah, *no*!" Lizzie cried.

Despite her warning call he touched the hot wood stove anyway and relearned a lesson he would not quickly forget. Lizzie comforted his bawl of pain, wiped his tears, patted away his hurts, and lovingly bandaged the blister, kissing away his lingering tears.

Because he was an adult with a childlike mind, Jem preferred the company of the young'uns to Lizzie's. He worshipfully tagged after the older boys the way they had once dogged his steps.

Jem listened to what was said, but he didn't understand.

At times he would laugh with wild abandon when there was clearly nothing funny.

At other times he would suffer a fit of weeping that would make Lizzie and the children teary-eyed in watching him and knowing the depth of the sorrow he could not express so that they could lighten his burden by sharing it with him.

March came in like a lion. And, as it prepared to go out like a lamb, Lizzie's birthday rolled around to mark off one more year.

The children in school had created festive greeting cards with Miss Abby's help.

Alton and Miss Abby had purchased a book of poetry.

And Linda Mathews baked a cake.

Unbidden, Lizzie's children stepped lively and helped with household chores, surprising their ma by doing up supper dishes while Lizzie lingered over her coffee. They told her it was her birthday treat, and because she was preoccupied, Lizzie did not expect ulterior motivation on their parts.

"Surprise!" the guests cried out as they arrived at Lizzie's farm for a party hastily planned and successfully kept secret.

Lizzie's eyes shone with tears of happiness as she saw the carefully selected mementos and realized that even though she sometimes felt lonely, she was, indeed, surrounded by those who loved and cared about her.

"Happy birthday, Ma!"

Lester, Thad, Maylon, and Harmony lined up to present her hugs and kisses.

Grinning happily, knowing that it was a jolly occasion, Jem fell in line, too. Bending his towering form to accept Lizzie's hug, he tendered his own, kissed her cheek, and said in a loud tone:

"MA–MA!"

The children laughed.

Alton, Miss Abby, and Brad shuffled uncomfortably.

Helplessly, her features crumpled with tears, Lizzie lowered her face and wept until her shoulders heaved with the heartbroken effort.

"Jeremiah's not to be pitied," Brad said and patted Lizzie's shoulder when the guests prepared to depart. "He has the sweet innocence of a child."

"And unless we are as little children, the Lord will not find favor in us," Alton added.

"Sometimes those who have the mind of a child seem to be the happiest of people," Miss Abby added. "We had such adults living with us at the Orphans' Home in Effingham. Truly, they were always smiling, always laughing, ready to give someone a hug, or extend affection to others. They considered everyone a friend. They didn't know what it is to have an enemy."

"That's true," Alton said. "They do seem to be happy folks."

Lizzie smiled sadly. "Yes, and I would suppose that they're blessedly ignorant of what all there is to worry about in this world, even though the Lord would have us be as unconcerned as the lilies of the field. . . ."

"There's always something to concern ourselves with. Taxes. Crops. Providing for others. Settin' by a little money for a rainy day. Growin' old alone."

"Those are things Jeremiah was once concerned with, too, and now he may know more content than he ever experienced before."

By the time nine months had passed, Lizzie held scarce hope that Jeremiah would regain knowledge that had faded away. She recognized Jem's new personality, one remarkably like the old, which made him a most agreeable individual to have present in the household.

Treated like one of the children, he now seemed to feel more at ease with Lizzie's young'uns than he did with her, and Lizzie's children, who'd once viewed him as their pa, now started to regard him as a sibling—as a brother to be taken care of and protected from harm as he'd once guided them in safe ways.

Lizzie wasn't really surprised when her bed grew empty one summer eve when Jeremiah, who'd had an enjoyable day tagging along with Lester, Maylon, and Thad, hated for the camaraderie to end, and he mutely climbed the rungs along with the boys.

Recognizing that the semblance of even being like a wife at all was a phase that had just ended, Lizzie chewed her lip and turned away, accepting it as she had all else.

With Jem absent from her bed and gone from her presence most of the days as he accompanied the boys to the field, sometimes Lizzie felt so much a widow that she had to stop and remind herself that Jeremiah was her husband. And she had to remind herself that he was her lawfully wedded mate, because he had grown to take the place of the child she'd longed for but had been unable to conceive and bear.

She realized, too, from absentminded remarks made by friends and neighbors that the fact of the situation sometimes escaped their minds, too. For they, too, seemed to sometimes forget that he wasn't just one of Lizzie's many children— another dependent who loved her, relied on her, revered her as his beloved Mama.

For so long now, Lizzie had not been a wife to Jem, nor he a husband to her. Not since before the accident.

With areas of his mind destroyed, Jeremiah Stone, who was as handsome as ever and still big and strong, was unable to fulfill passionate promises he no longer recalled having given to a pleasant woman he did not remember ever loving and desiring as a man, although he'd now come to adore as her child.

One year passed.

Then another.

As Lizzie's boys grew—with their maturing strength and Alton and Brad's guidance—the farm began to prosper again.

Lizzie was industrious around her household, and when she visited Brad's homestead, she instructed his daughters in the housekeeping arts as she had been well-taught by her own mother.

She scripted Fanny's prize receipts that had been handed down to her, and beamed with pride when Brad complimented her on what fine young ladies, appealing, talented, thrifty, and industrious the girls had become under her tutelage.

Lizzie was no less grateful for his and Alton's influence where her sons were concerned.

Because the two families were thrown together in their need, many a meal found them joined around the table that Lizzie had piled high with hearty, delectable foods that Brad's girls had helped to prepare, as little Harmony looked on and learned, too.

Socially, the two families tended to merge and blend at church, basket dinners, and community gatherings. To the neighbors' minds, Lizzie eventually came to realize that she and widower Brad Mathews had come to be thought of as a couple. A man and woman who belonged together and were invited jointly.

It was a caring relationship, with them linked in need and friendly affection in a manner always chaste.

Brad had never made an uncalled-for remark in her presence, and Lizzie was at ease with him, and he with her, because unspoken as it was, they seemed to have come to a mutual understanding.

Their relationship could never be more than it was. For Lizzie was wed to another man, even though that man

revered Brad Mathews as a pa and held him in the same
esteem presented Alton Wheeler, while Jeremiah had no
awareness of his legal or actual relationship to Lizzie, the
dependable woman he doted on and loved with a fullness
more expressive than the words he no longer knew how to
convey.

By day Lizzie knew that such pure love was enough.

But in the dead of the night, it was another matter. Her
traitorous dreams gave away the secret passions in her mind
that she dared not let take root in her heart for fear that the
subconscious fantasies would grow to become reality and
threaten what serenity and security she knew.

Thrilling as the dreams were while they lasted, such dreams
were almost nightmarish in the extent to which they left her
shaken, tormenting her over what her subconscious mind was
bringing up for her consideration.

But she mentioned the romantic dreams to no one, and
when each new day broke, she resolved that she would thrust
such thoughts far, far from mind during her waking hours
and pray to be delivered from such thrilling intrusions while
she slept.

And she scrupulously avoided occasions for improper
temptations to which she was no more immune, she sensed,
than was Brad Mathews, a handsome man, so long without a
woman . . . that perhaps he was as plagued with desirous
nighttime fantasies during slumber as she.

Summer days grew long and hot.

Blackberry season arrived, and with it came Lizzie's family's
plans to harvest the berries and peddle them to townspeople.

Out in the berry patch, briars pricked and snagged at
Lizzie's thin cotton gown, tearing at her tanned skin. The
choking scent of kerosene, to combat chiggers, wafted up
from the leggings she'd soaked in coal oil the night before.

Puffing for breath in the humid briarpatch, Lizzie stood on tiptoes, her fingertips clutching for the towering branch of lush timber berries hanging in dark purple clusters from the supple green briars—with thorns spiking out sharp as razors.

With steady, soft thumps the plump berries landed in the tin lard pail. As minutes passed the delectable fruit mounded higher and higher. The sun bore down. Lizzie wheezed a gust of breath, blowing a sticky wisp of stray hair away from her cheeks.

Zzzzzzzzzzzzzzzzzzzzzzzzzz!

Droning yellow jackets spiraled from a nest on the ground when Lizzie disturbed them.

The first insect hovered, shimmering in the hot, still air. With dumb instinct it darted close to Lizzie's face.

Emitting a squawk of alarm, Lizzie dropped her bucket of berries and flapped at the small insect. Another joined it. Wildly Lizzie flailed. She succeeded only in knocking her faded bonnet from her head. It hung down her back, fastened by sturdy ties knotted beneath her chin.

Before Lizzie thought to right the bonnet, she bent to rescue the berries. Scarcely had Lizzie leaned forward than she suffered an excruciating jab that brought pain tingling to her scalp. Instinctively she tried to twist away, but the bite of the briars sank deeper with every movement. Nearby, a long, soaring stalk no longer supported by the one Lizzie had disturbed, fell across her with a swish. It raked her across the cheek, falling to cling almost the entire length of her back. Sharp, needling briars nipped her with every shallow breath.

At first Lizzie struggled, but the briars twisted tighter every time she moved to extricate herself.

Finally, unable to bear the torment in the heat any longer, Lizzie ceased her struggles and surrendered to the tormenting thorns. Each time she tried to lift an arm to begin the process of loosening her long hair, another briar was drawn tighter elsewhere.

"Thad!" Lizzie cried. "Help! Lester—"

Again and again she bawled the children's names but no answers came, nor assistance.

As the sun steadily descended from a point high overhead, Lizzie realized how much time had passed. She finally heard footsteps accompanied by the thrashing of underbrush. Lizzie was too hot, weak, and exhausted to do more than croak at her rescuer.

"Mama's over here!"

Lizzie was not expecting her rescuer to be Brad Mathews.

"It *is* you!" Brad gasped. "I stopped by your cabin but found no one at home. I waited, thinking you'd return. Then I heard your cries. Land sakes, you're trapped tight as a bug in a web."

"Have you a penknife in your pocket?"

"Yes," Brad admitted, then cast a nervous glance over Lizzie's old, worn gown.

"My hair. You'll h–have to cut my hair to set me free, Brad."

"No, Miss Lizzie!" Brad protested. "Not your hair. We can't cut your beautiful hair."

Lizzie felt about to wilt from the heat and weariness and the sunburn on her cheeks.

"It will grow back . . ."

Lizzie turned slightly, rolling her eyes to meet Brad's. A vicious scratch had laid across her cheek, forming a bright red jagged line where droplets of blood had welled to the surface and dried.

"I can't cut your hair, Miss Lizzie. *Won't* cut your hair. Trust me not to hurt you any more than necessary. A bit of

178

pain now will be less to bear than months of agony when you confront yourself in a looking glass."

With his sharp pocketknife Brad cut the nearby briars to purchase room in which to work. He hacked more briars and drew them away, then snipped off the stalks so that only the leafy tips, fuzzy with sharp miniature briars, clasped tightly to her hair.

She took a step, then limped as a thorn that had worked its way into her shoe sank into her flesh. She hobbled from the patch.

"Poor Miss Lizzie. You look plumb tuckered. You carry your pail, Miss Lizzie, 'n' I'll tote you. You're none too steady on your feet."

"I can walk . . . I think."

"I think not. I won't have you swoonin' into another bramble patch from which I'll be called to rescue you," Brad informed her and swooped her into his arms.

Lizzie managed a weak grin. "My knight in . . . faded chambray. . . ."

Brad smiled back, his face inches from her own sunburned cheeks. "Milady in ragged calico. . . ."

Together they laughed, but the merry sound was suffocated by their quick gasps of realization that spoke their sudden acknowledgment of physical awareness as Brad clasped her in his arms. She was aware of the heat radiating from his chest, and the burning imprint of his arms as he cradled her behind the knees and across the small of her back.

Silence spiraled, making their breath seem loud in the still afternoon. Suddenly words failed them both, making their private thoughts seem all the more evident to each other.

When Brad stumbled as he bore her along, Lizzie was helpless not to tighten her arms around his neck. He supported her, and his arm beneath her hips and the tucking folds of her skirt behind her knees seemed to burn with power and life.

"I—I can walk," Lizzie weakly suggested, more to free herself from the frightening sensations than to escape from his arms.

Brad shook his head but avoided Lizzie's eyes as if to win the right not to forfeit a cargo precious to him, by ignoring the opportunity. Yet, decency seemed to cry out to him to offer a suitable explanation and excuse.

"It's only a short way to the clearing," Brad said. "The ground is so rough here, Lizzie. Weak as you are from the heat and your struggles, I don't want to risk your fallin' 'n' mayhap hurtin' yourself further."

Almost no sooner had Brad's explanation been given, than he himself hooked a foot on a wild grape vine that snaked across the forest floor before it shinnied up a nearby tree. He staggered, with effort caught his balance, only to lose it again.

Reeling, he pitched into another tiny clearing where he ungallantly dropped a nervously giggling Lizzie to the ground.

Her shocked laughter turned to lamentation as she landed with a hard jolt that caused her teeth to clack together as she made contact with the earth.

"Ouch! Oooooooh," Lizzie cried softly. "My head!" Gingerly she fingered the back of her head and tried to sit up. In her advanced state of exhaustion, the effort was too much. She collapsed to the ground, panting for breath, her eyes closed against the glaring sunlight.

"What's the matter?" Brad asked.

"There's still a briar in my hair somewhere," she murmured and lifted a weary arm to discover it but found she hadn't the strength as her arm flopped back to her side.

"Let me do it," Brad suggested. He sat up, winded, quite breathless from carrying Lizzie.

"I'm heavier than I realized," Lizzie blurted. "I'm sorry."

"Apologies refused. 'Tis merely a matter of me being unused to carrying a burden heavier than your Miss Harmony, 'n' her a young lass already."

He fell silent and his stocky fingers plucked at the briar stickers lodged in Lizzie's sunburned scalp.

"Ouuuuuuuuch!" Lizzie whispered, flinching.

"Sorry, darlin'. Hold still a moment longer and it'll be over."

"Are you f—finished?" she inquired as a long moment passed and she was excruciatingly aware of his nearness as he knelt beside her, his chest grazing her back as he worked to extricate the burr of briars.

". . . Just about."

"You needn't finish," she said, struggling to arise. "We'd best be goin'."

Brad laid a gentle hand on her arm. "You don't have to flee from me, woman. I won't hurt you."

"I—I know, Brad, but—but—"

"But if felt good, didn't it? It felt different havin' you in my arms, Lizzie, instead of havin' to be content with just givin' you a hand up, or a hand down, as you get into or out of a carriage or wagon."

Brad's voice seemed to tremble as he made the private admission. He touched Lizzie's chin and made her face him.

"Shameless as it is o' me to admit it, Lizzie, it felt powerful wonderful holdin' you in my arms. Like the culmination of all of my daydreams."

Lizzie tensed at his touch. Her skin suddenly seemed to warm ten degrees. Her pulse galloped to a staccato rhythm.

181

Rapid as a hummingbird's wing, her heart seemed to flutter beneath her faded, almost tissuey calico bodice.

"D—don't say such things, Brad!" Lizzie begged, even as a maverick corner of her heart cherished the tender admission.

"'N' why not?" he challenged. "It's the thought layin' on both of our minds. You'll be lyin' to me, woman, if you dare to deny it. I know that you want me every bit as much as I've come to love and desire you."

Lizzie turned her face away from him.

"Yes, and the shame's mine to bear that I can't deny it, Brad, for it *did* feel good in the arms of a man."

"Not just the arms of a man, Lizzie. But in the arms of a fellow who *loves* you. Wants to care for you. Be there for you and yours always. Lizzie, I adore you."

"Brad, shush! Don't say things you'll regret—that we'll regret."

"And why not? Lizzie, everyone knows already that we're in love with one another!"

"Brad, *please!*" Lizzie begged and closed her eyes.

She was praying for strength. Brad misunderstood. He seemed to believe that when her eyelids sank shut and she shuddered, lifting her face heavenward, she was offering him her kiss.

She was startled by the quick, light buss that landed on her mouth.

Lizzie's eyes flipped open and as she turned, shaken, alarmed, her lips collided with Brad's mouth. With his intent, his warm lips clung to Lizzie's as she struggled to get away and find a hasty retreat.

But retreat was not something Brad would allow right then. And retreat was, an instant later, impossible, for Lizzie had no further desire to escape what she'd suddenly found within Brad Mathews's loving arms.

She was lost in the perfection of his kiss, basking in the promise of his embrace. But a moment later the wave of warmth that had swept over her dissipated in the cold face of reality.

Oh, dear God, she thought and shuddered. *What if someone saw us stealing kisses, exchanging an embrace? The children? Jeremiah? One of the neighbors?*

"Please! Stop! Oh, Brad, if you care for me at all—don't do this to me, I'm beggin' you—"

A stunned Brad released her, although his hands still grazed the tips of her shoulder as he held her at arm's length.

"Please, don't ruin it by apologizin', Lizzie, or wanting me to beg your pardon. Don't say you're sorry, especially when we both know that we're not. If you say anything, my darling, utter only the words that will make me the happiest of men. Agree that you will marry me. Be my wife!"

Lizzie gaped at him. Her mouth worked, but, for a horrible moment, no sound came out.

"But Brad!" she finally found her voice, although it was breathless and thin. "I can't do that. I *am* married. I'm Jeremiah's wife. You know that as well as I. I'm married to another."

He drew a deep breath. "In name only. We both know that—everyone in the neighborhood realizes it."

"Regardless, there's no putting aside the fact that Jem's my husband."

"He thinks he's your *child.*"

"He's still my husband," Lizzie repeated limply.

"Don't be obstinate! How long has it been, Lizzie," Brad demanded, "since Jeremiah has performed as a husband to you?"

Lizzie's face flamed. She tried to turn away, but in his

intentness he clutched her wrist and turned her right back to him.

"That's a question you've no right to ask, Mister Mathews," Lizzie sputtered in an indignant tone, "and that I have no intention of answering!"

He gave a haggard, bitter laugh. "Nor do I have to await your answer, Lizzie," Brad pointed out, "because I know exactly how long 'tis been! Since at the latest the day of the accident or however long before. . . ."

"So what am I supposed to do?" Lizzie asked in a woebegone tone. "What do you want of me?"

Brad's anger of the moment before was forgotten. He reached out to cup her flushed, sun-reddened cheek. "Marry me, Lizzie. Let me be your husband, be my beloved wife. I do love you so. And I know that you care about me and mine, the way I do about your family."

"Yes, but Jem—"

Brad stared into his strong hands. Then he lifted his eyes to meet Lizzie's unwavering gaze.

"Put Jem aside," he suggested in a quiet tone, in a voice so faint that Lizzie almost had to strain her ears to hear as the breeze all but drowned him out. "Quietly divorce him so that you are free to marry me. People—strangers—may talk. But it would die down after a while. 'N' those close to us would understand and not be scandalized by what is best for both of us. They know what's become of Jeremiah's mind since the accident. We'd never shut him from our lives, Lizzie. He'd always have a home with us. We'd care for him like one of the children. You know how Jeremiah admires me, and how I've come to love him like my son. He'd be happy with us all together, Lizzie, 'n' so would we. We could be a whole family, 'stead of two halves, waitin' to be made one."

Lizzie's thoughts spun.

There was so much logic behind his rational arguments. Lizzie knew that it was a line of reasoning that would not be refuted by their family and friends. But just because it was accepted by the world did not mean that it would be acceptable to the Lord—that she would be excused from fulfilling her sacred promise freely given.

In her silence Brad found hope, and his lips met Lizzie's in a convincing kiss, so tender, so ripe with hope, and sweet with promise that Lizzie began to melt.

"I'm asking you to marry me, but I don't want the answer now. I won't even accept an answer at the moment. I want you to think on it . . . dwell on it . . . pray over the matter. Decide a little later, Lizzie. I'll return at another time for your decision. When can I—?"

Hurriedly, awkwardly, Lizzie arose from the ground. She gripped her bonnet, clutched her bucket, gathered up her skirt to reveal neat ankles, and turned to scamper away.

"When, Lizzie?" Brad cried after her. "When can I come for your decision?"

His plaintive call reached out to her, but Lizzie would not answer—could not answer. She already knew the decision. She knew what her troubled heart wanted. And she knew what the Lord God desired of her. So there was no question, really. And there was no answer but one.

The answer was . . . had to be . . . NO!

Lizzie staggered into the dim cabin, reeling. As her eyes grew accustomed to the dark room, she leaned against the washstand, trying to counter the faint-headed symptoms of heat exhaustion combined with having been thoroughly kissed by a man she loved and wanted but would be denied until the Lord ordained that it was right and good for them to be together.

She ladled a drink from the water bucket, but the tepid

water would not go down. Her stomach recoiled and she spat into the slop jar.

Holding onto the wall for balance, she entered the dining room. There, propped against the coal oil lamp positioned in the center of her round oak table was a slate left over from the school term.

Squeezing his words to make room for the message, Lester had chalked the communication that they'd had great luck picking berries and that they'd returned home to hitch the wagon and take the berries to town.

Lizzie sighed and set the slate aside. She felt relieved that the young'uns were not there to witness her distress.

Leisurely Lizzie bathed.

Then, with the time presented her, she washed her long hair, toweled it dry, and dressed in a fresh, neat frock. She spread the damp towel across her shoulders, fanning her tresses likewise, and stepped outside for the breeze to dry her hair.

Evening birds chirped nearby.

Birds flitted overhead. A bluejay cried warning, then swooped, darting, at Beauregard, Jeremiah's Blue Tick hound dog, who was growing crippled with age and was content to romp after a mute, confused Jem, where once they had expertly hunted together.

Lizzie slipped into the house, noting the unusual quiet. She plucked her Bible from its resting place on the mantel and then returned outside to the serene outdoors and its natural majesty.

Sighing, she seated herself and opened the Good Book. As she knew in her heart, her eyes encountered the familiar guiding words of wisdom inspired by the Creator, to affirm her decision formulated in her mind even as her human heart rebelled and sought another, an easier, a more appealing way.

She couldn't cast Jem aside. Nor, could she spurn his love once given—indeed a love bestowed upon her yet, although in a different way. The fact remained unaltered: Jeremiah was her husband. Before God and their friends, she had promised to forsake all others. She had tendered a vow to cherish him and care for him in sickness and in health until death did them part.

She could not accept Brad's proposal of marriage, bringing such travesty to him, anymore than she could agree and in the process cast such an aspersion on herself.

Ah, the weaknesses of a man . . . with their ruination so often coming through their desire to possess that special woman even when it was wrong and they knew it, but they stubbornly refused to be denied the pleasures they sought.

Eve. . . .

Delilah. . . .

Bathsheba. . . .

Tamar. . . .

And so many others. . . .

Well, she would not be a temptress leading a good man astray, placing his feet on the path leading to his downfall, and eroding his faith as he followed his will, convincing himself, rationalizing that it was right, even when it was in direct opposition to the Word of God as he knew and understood it.

She would be strong in her faith.

Strong enough for the both of them.

When Lizzie heard the clop of approaching hoofbeats, she at first thought it was Lester bearing the children home. But when she noticed the absence of the accompanying creak and thunk of wagon wheels, she knew that a stranger approached on horseback. It was Brad!

Lizzie met Brad at the yard gate, swallowing tears.

"I can't put Jeremiah aside and wed you, Brad. Not when I vowed before God to take Jem as my husband for better or for worse, richer or poorer, in sickness and in health, for ever and ever until eternity parts us."

Brad nodded as he remembered his own vows once given to Emily, and perfectly fulfilled by him as he'd lovingly nursed her until she'd drawn her final breath.

"I can't divorce Jeremiah and repeat those same vows to you, Brad, all the while knowin' that I didn't fulfill my promise to Jeremiah, or to the Lord. I'd be a liar, 'n' worse, an adulteress. We'd make a cuckold of Jeremiah. I love you, Brad, too much to agree to marry you, even as we both desire it."

Reminded of the tenets of his faith and the inarguable facts underscored by sacred Scriptures, his weak moments of temptation had passed.

"You're right, Lizzie, even though in one way I'm heart-broke in your denying me, while in another I'm grateful that you're finding me worthy of Christian exhortation."

Lizzie's eyes swam with tears. "Please don't hate me for doing what I know is right."

Brad stared at her, aghast.

"Hate you, Lizzie?" he cried, his tone faint with incredulity. "Your refusin' me only somehow makes me love you all the more, what with an even deeper recognition of what a fine woman of faith you are to put His will ahead of our wants. If anything, Lizzie, you could hate me for the inappropriate askin'."

"Never, Brad. I could never hate you. And I'll always cherish knowing that I'm still appealing and attractive to a handsome man. For that knowledge, Brad, I'll always have a special love for you—and gratefulness for the friend to me you've always been."

"Oh, Lizzie," Brad said. He drew her into his arms. He held her close. But it was a gesture lacking of passion, as it was filled with the purity of love and the fellowship of caring that had always been theirs.

"My feelings will remain unchanged for you, Lizzie," Brad promised. "We won't let this painful day come between us. I'll always be there for you, Lizzie, ready to lend assistance anytime you've the need. Jem's a lucky man," Brad said, "even though he may not realize it. If only he knew . . . if only he knew."

"Someday he will," Lizzie murmured. "'N' then we'll have nothing to be ashamed for, Brad. And there'll be a heap o' consolation in havin' done the right thing."

"Doing right's not easy. But, it's . . . right," Brad murmured. "And in your doing the godly thing and insisting that I do, too, if anything, Lizzie, my love for you has grown and so has my respect for your word well-given." He paused. "Just as you refused to cast Jeremiah aside and null your word, if the Lord ordains that someday we shall stand side by side before His altar and extend our vows to each other, then I can trust in the surety of your oath to me, with it unmarred by the haunting knowledge that you have broken a vow, and put aside another, who also received your sacred promise."

"Oh, Brad . . ."

"And if it be our lot to never know the sweet fulfillment of our love, then it will be enough for me just to claim such a fine, strong woman as my friend, and a shining example of Christian womanhood for my daughters."

Brad made preparations to leave. He tipped his hat in a gesture of respect and reined his horse around.

"I'll be praying for you and yours, Miss Lizzie."

"As I shall for you and your kin, Brad."

Lizzie stood near the maple tree in the front lawn and

watched Brad ride away. Her eyes filled with tears. By the time the children returned home she was openly weeping.

Like a shell of herself she moved around the dim kitchen preparing their meal, grateful for the shadowy flickerings of the coal-oil lamps that hid the ravages of her bitter tears.

Maylon, Lester, and Thad nervously regarded her woman's tears and bore the discovery in stoic silence, unable to discern words of comfort. Harmony tried to cheer her mother, but Lizzie was beyond consolation even though none of them could conclude what was troubling her and dared not inquire.

One by one, her children confronted a broken Lizzie who seemed beyond recognition, a haunted woman, a stranger to them in her deep, unidentifiable grief.

Individually they slipped away, unable to bear the sorrow of the cheerful woman so steeped in unnamed grief that they feared that she would find it within herself to laugh no more.

Lester . . .

Maylon . . .

Thad . . .

Harmony . . .

Each beloved child tendered confused good-nights, then silently blended into the darkness as Lizzie sat in the shadows and wept from the wellspring of her disappointment.

Jeremiah regarded her with large, troubled eyes that knew of her grief even as he did not understand it and would not, even had she troubled to take the time to explain her anguish.

Slowly, gently, the last in line he put his arms around her and laid his cheek against her shoulder, patting awkwardly, clumsily, on her back.

"Ma—ma!" he whispered hoarsely. "Ma—ma!"

Biting her lip, pinching her eyes against her tears, Lizzie crushed him to her and held him hard, but the tears only increased.

For herself.

For him.

But as she held him close, and he crooned, "Ma—ma!" so tenderly and clumsily patted her, the joy returned as did the memories.

"Be content . . . be happy," she whispered the admonishment as her lips were pressed close to Jem's cheek.

"Ma—ma!" Jem said in a happier, relieved tone, and settled for patting her one last time before he edged away.

After stealing another quick hug she released him, and being mollified, Jeremiah followed the path of Lester, Maylon, and Thad, climbing the rungs to the attic.

"Oh, Jem . . . ," Lizzie whispered as she watched him go and disappear from sight.

Thump!

Lizzie heard Jem settle onto his pallet in the attic up above. Boosting herself from the rocking chair, she made her way through the darkness, drew back the quilts, and slipped into her lonely bed.

Although they were parted, she knew that Jeremiah was still hers. And she was his. For ever and ever . . . until death did them part.

An exhausted Lizzie Stone drifted away until she was claimed by the refreshing slumber of content and happy souls, those at peace with themselves, and in obedience to the Lord. . . .